*Dedication to my beautiful daughter Poppy, who has believed and encouraged me from the beginning of my writing journey.
Love Dad.

Welcome to the weird and wonderful world of my tragic short stories.
An eclectic collection of tales aimed to encourage reading to a generation where instant gratification is a must.

The Book of Short Tragic Stories
Volume One

By *Kevin Gargini*

Love to Die

His skin was stained red with blood. Jake was full, he'd never felt so content. This was the start of a new chapter in his life. He was now a young man and could no longer rely on his parents to feed him, it was taking a toll on them. Jake had plans on going back to the old country, where it had all started. Jake was a budding historian and wanted to walk in the steps of his ancestors. He wanted to breathe the same air and find the abandoned burnt remains of his family's castle. He wanted to go back to Hunedoara in Romania, a city in the region of Transylvania.

Jake had just made his first kill, a twelve-month-old lamb. His parents were extremely protective of him and always provided bottled blood for Jake to devour. He only recently began asking his parents where this blood had come from, but they always avoided the question.

Jake was one of nine children; however they were all older and had fled the nest to live their own lives. Jake was a popular lad but missed out on a lot of the social events due to his parents protective nature. He was handsome, with short brown hair and had just had his seventeenth birthday. He was on the Eve of adulthood and was more than ready to become a man.

He lived in Loxwood, just on the outskirts of Horsham where Jake lived with his parents on a small holding. It was a beautiful place with a couple of acres of land, which was enough for a vegetable garden and some livestock. Mainly chickens and lambs with a couple of pigs. His parents kept themselves to themselves and rarely had contact with too many locals.

Jake was told that he and his father were called moroi and his mother was a moroaica. Some say that in Romanian folklore they are type of phantom, but to Jake they were just a normal family, because that was all he really knew. His family had a
saying,
"The less you know, the better you sleep".

As Jake got older, he began craving for something other than animal blood, it was enough to keep him alive but didn't fulfil his wants and desires. It was like drinking a healthy smoothie every day, but really craving a huge double cheeseburger.

Before Jake left the fold, his parents wanted to train him in the art of killing. This sounds awful but to them it was normal and in their DNA. Jake had to learn first and foremost, how to fly. A peculiar concept considering they didn't have wings, but quite normal for his parents. They could fly with the power of their mind, a belief in their own abilities had to be strong for their supernatural powers to work. Jake was taught how to meditate, a belief in the existence of a core or true Self was critical.

Once flying was accomplished, he had to learn how to become invisible. This was a short-term solution, so he was taught how to stay in the shadows, how to remain silent and only use invisibility as a last precaution, as it would drain his strength.

Learning how to kill and dispose of a body was less complicated. A cut to the wrist to make it look like suicide and not to be greedy was key. Picking victims had to be researched in a gruesome way. Choosing loners, depressants and the mentally handicapped was in someways a huge battle of morality, but to become immortal the consumption of human blood was a necessity.

After being bottle fed and then killing livestock, Jake had to take a human. He was nervous and scared; he had done his homework on his victim but was worried about being seen by a witness. When the big day was just 24 hours away, he was briefed for the last time by his parents.

The day came and Jake got ready, his first victim was a teacher from his old school. He didn't like her, she was mean to the students and was rude to other staff members. Her name was Ms Miles, she lived alone and was childless, she didn't even own a pet. A very bitter person who was just angry all of the time.

Jake went for a walk near to her house around 9pm, he then used his invisibility to avoid any cameras or Ring doorbells. He watched Ms Miles through her back window until she went upstairs to bed. He gained entry with the help of some locksmith tools his father lent him, and he crept upstairs. Silently he entered her bedroom, Ms Miles was asleep, Jake used a cloth with chloroform on and just held it still near her nose. Ms Miles breathed the sweet smelling chemicals and was knocked unconscious within minutes. A small prod confirmed it in her lifeless body.

Jake pulled out a silver-coloured razor blade, held Ms Miles' arm up and made a two inch incision. Straight away the blood flowed effortlessly like a leak in a dam and Jake drank the metallic nectar like he was downing a pint on a sunny day. His father taught him that he could only drink for one minute, that would be enough for him and leave the body with enough blood, so it doesn't look suspicious.

Jake enjoyed every drop, he then lay her arm down on the bed and placed the razor blade in her other hand, a perfect suicide scene for some poor sod to find. Jake left and made his way back home carefully. He was greeted by his parents when he arrived like he had just graduated from Oxford, they were proud as punch.

In the morning, Jake contemplated on what he'd done, he'd basically murdered someone for his dinner. His father tried to reassure him by explaining that it's who they are and that a despicable person is now deceased. After Jake's English breakfast, including black pudding he had come to terms with last night's events and went and met some friends.

One kill a week was allowed for Jake, otherwise the police would get suspicious. He also had to move around different areas otherwise it would look like the suicide pact in Bridgend in 2007 when 23 men died in one year. They didn't want the media to get involved.

As time went on, Jake perfected his new skills and at the age of twenty he was given the opportunity to travel around Europe. He spent time in Paris, Frankfurt, Berlin, Prague and then Budapest. He fed from over one hundred people and felt amazing. He was stronger and quicker than he'd ever been and had turned into a man that caught the eye of the ladies.

After two years of traveling, Jake finally made it to Romania, his ancestral homeland. Straight away he felt like he belonged there, people were friendly and the country was beautiful. He made his way to the Transylvanian region and started his search for his family's castle.

Whilst in the local library he noticed an elderly man staring at him. He didn't know or recognise him, but the man just nodded at him in acknowledgment. Later that day whilst ordering some food he met a young woman. Her name was Mina, she was beautiful, she had long dark hair and a kind pretty smile.

Jake fell in love instantly. He'd never felt this way and it scared him. Mina was a student in Brasov at the University of Transylvania, she was in her last year. After weeks of trying, he eventually got her to agree on a date. They went to Ograda, a restaurant in the town square, it had a folk-style charm and played melodious tunes in the background.

They ate the traditional homemade sausages, drank wine and talked for hours. It was an incredible night and Jake knew he would never find another like her. That night he decided Mina was the woman he was going to marry. After that night they were inseparable, and after a few months they moved to a small farm together.

During this period Mina knew nothing about Jake's lifestyle, he kept it well hidden, and Mina was none the wiser. Jake would make up reasons to disappear in the evenings, and visiting the gym or going for a run seemed to work. Mina was a big reader so would often lose track of time reading a novel, she was planning to write her own one day.

It took Jake a long time, but he eventually found the location of his ancestral castle. There wasn't much left other than a few outbuildings and ruins that were fire damaged. It was overgrown and looked as though it had been deserted for centuries. Something touched him though and he felt a spiritual presence. With Mina pregnant now, Jake had a choice, to fulfil his legacy or to spend a mortal life with Mina.

Jake didn't want to make that decision straight away so continued to live a double life, a murdering blood sucker and a husband and father of now three children. Killing became second nature, but the taste of human blood was becoming boring, but to maintain immortality he had to do it. Meanwhile his relationship with Mina was just getting better and better, she was a wonderful mother and a fantastic wife.

On Jake's 50th birthday he made a decision. To live forever and outlive everyone he knew and loved or to be mortal and die when the time was right. He didn't want to live without Mina, and he certainly didn't want to see his children grow old and die. He also made a decision not to tell his children about his gift or curse, however you view it. He thought that as they were only half his they may not have the same desires as he did. So, that night he made a vow to himself that the killings and the blood consumption would stop.

For the love of his wife and his children, he decided to give up living forever and to be a mortal man. This was like a drug addict going cold turkey, it hurt his body, he felt his body was changing and he lost a lot of weight. It was noticeable to his wife, and she was incredibly worried about him. Mina almost took him to hospital, but he talked her out of it, he was so close to going back to his blood sport.

He eventually confessed his gruesome life to Mina, he told her everything. Poor Mina, such a beautiful lady, she didn't say anything, she just stared into the sky. Jake was heartbroken, he thought his news had destroyed her. Jake picked a knife up from the table, said sorry to Mina and was going to plunge the knife into his own heart. Mina, saw what he was doing and rushed to him to wrestle the knife away, but in the scuffle the knife entered Mina's stomach.

Mina fell to the floor and bled heavily from her terminal wound. Jake was going to lose his wife, the mother of his children, he was in pieces. He held onto Mina's stomach and attempted to stop the bleeding. It wouldn't stop; she was dying. Jake looked into her eyes, he told her he loved her and that he couldn't lose her.

Jake with tears in his eyes held Mina up, and for the first time in his life and without knowing if it would work, he bite into Mina's neck. She squealed as his teeth sank into her mortal flesh and he fed, but just for a few seconds. With blood dripping from his mouth, he kissed Mina and said, "Please trust me". With the little strength Mina had she looked at Jake as he brought his wrist close to her mouth. Mina paused, looked at Jake and said, "I knew, I always knew, you fool".
She then bit into his wrist and fed off her husband's blood, she drank until Jake couldn't take anymore.

Jake fell to the floor in a heap, Mina lay still, like a stone. Jake eventually pulled himself up and moved over to his beloved. "Mina, Mina", he said. Mina's eyes were closed she had his blood smudged on her face, he held her head up, "Mina, please.
Please wake up ", he screamed.
Mina's eyes opened; they glowed back at Jake. He smiled at her and apologised for everything.

Mina had survived, but it came at a price. To live, Mina had to accept her new life, her life as a vampiress. The Queen of Darkness. In the distance there was the sound of thunder and then a bolt of lightning shot down.
 It was all about to start again....

The End

Her Name Was Chaos

Chaos was a nightmare. She missed classes, turned up late
to appointments. Chaos was chaotic. She lived by her own
rules. She didn't walk or run she floated around like Willo
the Wisp. It was though she didn't have a care in the
world.
But she did! There was something about her, she was
mysterious. She would travel around listening to chilled
out music on her iPods while checking out homemade
jewellery at craft shows.

Chaos would buy secondhand clothes from all over and
always looked great. She seemed to prefer her own
company and other girls admired her from a distance. She
was 19, athletic thin build but she never exercised. Chaos
was beautiful, not your typical stunner, she was quirky
and witty. I had spent some time with her in pubs, clubs,
classes and the canteen but I didn't really know her. I'm
not sure anyone did, but she was definitely on my mind.

Why am I telling you this?

Chaos wasn't her real name, obviously. This was a name
my friends and I called her due to her lifestyle. We liked
her and we loved her vibe, it seemed to fit in with our life

in Brighton. University was great, I think. It went by in a blur. The problem with having a group of students as mates is that every night at least one person wants to go out and get drunk. I was usually up for this, which didn't help my studies.

Chaos came out with us on occasions, usually the big nights when a bunch of us went out. When we were all out, we would often lose each other and meet up irregularly throughout the night. It seemed to work and Chaos would disappear for ages, usually off her head. I had a girlfriend, but I really liked Chaos. She wasn't exactly girlfriend material, but I wanted to look after her, I was always attracted to fallen angels. I guess I was worried about her, she didn't have any ambitions or future plans, it was a little strange.

One day a rumour was going around that Chaos had been arrested. This wasn't out of the ordinary as we were students in Brighton, and she probably got caught with some weed by some bored anal police officer.

After meeting up with her at the pub she said it was for shoplifting, she'd taken some makeup that she couldn't afford. However, she had been charged and had a court date. At the time we thought she could have gotten away with a police caution, but we didn't push her.

Two weeks later she was arrested again, she said she had been hungry and stole some food. All fairly harmless, it seemed.

Court.

Being students and having time on our hands we thought we'd support her at the magistrate's court. Oh boy, were we in for a surprise. The magistrate's court was a dour place and we had to hang about for a few hours, but eventually made our way into the public gallery. The magistrates sat high on their thrones, judging the plebs.

We weren't exactly prepared for what we heard. The clerk of the court read out her charges; theft x5, being found on enclosed premises x2, theft from person and resist arrest.

Wow, what on earth was going on, it was like being hit by Mike Tyson. Surely, they had the wrong person, it was ridiculous, this couldn't be Chaos.
Chaos pleaded guilty to all charges, before being sentenced a man stood up and said they had been working with her to help her drug issues, but she had relapsed. The Magistrates took little pity and sent her to prison for six months. Chaos wouldn't make eye contact with us as she was led away, I could see a few tears running down her face, I think at this point I'd briefly fallen in love with her. I just wanted to hug her and take her for a wonder down the Lanes.

We left the court and had a debrief down the pub, we were all a bit shaken, and a pint always helps. We needed to piece together what had happened. We had a plan; speak to her other friends, her work and try and find her address.

We paired up to make our enquiries, with a plan to meet in the evening to discuss our findings (down the pub, of course).

Chaos didn't have a job, she was fired months ago, she was caught stealing, none of her friends knew much more than we did but we found her accommodation. She was living in squat with several others who didn't look too well and were economical with their information. We were able to discover a bit more. The problem with drug addicts is that they only think about themselves, their next hit is all that matters. However, when we reconvened, we could form some kind of lifestyle that she was living.

Smack!

Turns out she was living in a squat with a bunch of musicians/ drug users. They would busk for money and get high at night. Poor Chaos was introduced to heroin and quickly became an addict. It was sort of making sense, the more we drank the more we understood.

The secondhand clothes, the homemade jewellery, disheveled hair, the tardiness , and floating around like a butterfly. She wasn't floating around in a poetic fashion she was high on heroin. None of us had seen it. The mysterious girl had to remain anonymous because she was leading two separate lives.

One life was being a student and studying, the other was hanging around with street urchins making money any which way they could and getting high. I was absolutely gutted. I was upset she didn't trust me, but I sort of got it. She felt normal with us, she was a student at university with likeminded people, and we helped her feel normal.

I never saw Chaos again. I still think about her. There was a story in the newspaper a year later, that she had been imprisoned again, but the publicity was down to her family were.

Her father was a Viscount and lived in a huge country mansion. Chaos had it all but rejected it. Her mother had died when Chaos was thirteen and that broke her. Her father had paid thousands of pounds on a Shrink but it didn't work. The family had tried all sorts to help her but Chaos couldn't be saved. She'd had a good education but she was beaten by the pain, heart broken.

The last thing I heard about Chaos was from another newspaper article. I was at work on a break, flicking through a red top, and I froze, I couldn't move.
The article was about her funeral and the paparazzi went to town taking snaps of the rich and famous who attended. She was only 27.

Her name was Lily, but she'll always be Chaos to me.

The End

Based on true events.

The Human Downfall

The rain hasn't stopped since the machines took control of the earth. The whole city is now underwater, the only way of getting around the once bustling place is by the plastic ferries that are forced upon people to get to the work houses. Unless of course people want to take their chances by swimming or making their own rafts. This however was extremely dangerous. The machines would randomly electrocute certain areas just so any non-compliant behaviour was stamped out quickly and brutally. Half of the population in Antara City had died, most have been killed.

It all started in 2015, a young man called Eddie Temmis had a dream where all low level domestic duties were taken care of by machines and they would slowly enter people's lives as easily as the kettle did. Gradually items such as the robot lawnmower, vacuum and clothes folding machines adorned most homes, as frequently as dishwashers and washing machines. Eventually the overall cost of these luxury item's became affordable, due to Capitalism and supply and demand. The more companies producing machines not only pushed the price down, they also cut corners and use inferior products.

Eddie or Eddie the Terrorist as he became known, was a nice lad, ambitious, intelligent and wanted his inventions to help and assist people in their daily lives. People needed help with domestic chores because they were boring and time consuming. especially as the populations average working week had gone up from 40 hours to 52 hours. Instead of working for the necessities of food, clothing and shelter, people were now working longer and harder to afford these Smart appliances so their lives at home would be easier.

What they didn't realise, was they were no longer working for one company, they were now working for the two or three credit cards companies or banks they owed money to. A credit card debt weighed people down like a ball and chain. Interest payments were the only part they could usually afford, so the debt never went away and they would be working forever. This kept shareholders happy because they were getting richer and the divide between the rich and poor was becoming larger and larger.

Eddie wasn't content with household machines, he wanted bigger and better inventions. Flying cars becoming a regular was a dream of his since he was a little child, especially after seeing movies like The Fifth Element. Self drive cars, planes , spaceships and helicopters became normal by the year 2038. There was no need for pilots, taxi or coach drivers or even astronauts.

Opposable thumbs were the humans massive benefits all through evolution, as is their willing and ability to learn so there were always jobs that needed humans. Gradually massive warehouses on the outskirts of large towns and cities were common place. They had strict confidentiality policies so the businesses were always kept private.

Humans were always susceptible to believing what they are told via their screens and what the politicians want us to believe. A worldwide experiment was conducted in 2019 where an alleged virus had become a pandemic. The population's movements were restricted, curfews were put in place and shopping was done from home. Amazingly this experiment worked, the general population were only to happy if not eager to tell tales on each other for the sake of National Safety, reminiscent of the Secret Service in countries like Germany and Russia, where speaking out against your leaders was treated as treason. How did the governments know? Easy, they convinced the population that it was for the greater good and 95% believed it.

Jimmy was in the 5%, he knew it was all a conspiracy to control people, but he and his followers were given all sorts of names like conspiracy theorists, the far right, racist, sexiest, homophobic, you name it, every negative label was pushed onto them to break their legitimate beliefs.

As each year went by, control was being forced more often and people's rights were being taken away. All happening in front of the eyes of the people, but the powers to be were liars, and to fight against it would put you in prison. Text messages, phone calls , emails and any other form of communication were monitored in these huge warehouses.

By 2050, the machines were so intelligent that they were now breaking into the government, and being voted in for cabinet roles. They were gradually infiltrating the system in plain sight. It was a silent invasion which the current powers allowed because of the massive financial gains they were receiving via these huge companies.

By 2056, the machines had all but grabbed power and the population became slaves. Due to the huge running costs and extra fuel use, the climate had changed drastically and it rained everyday. The machines claimed that they were working on plans to find alternatives, but that never materialised.

Even at this point, Jimmy and his followers were still ousted by their neighbours and family members so they had to live underground, which wasn't easy. The flooding was causing crops to fail so people were eating canned food products produced in giant factories using synthetic materials and chemicals.

Humans had become slaves to the environment they invented. Jimmy and his followers will continue to fight against the system, but they will never win, once the process started it was already too late.

Self-destruction in the journey of discovery.

The End

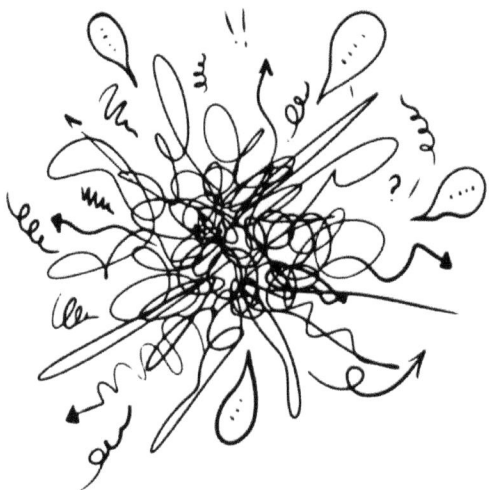

The Stranger

A stranger sat at her table claiming to be her soulmate.

The man, elderly wearing an old suit and with a side parting with the little hair he had left, read this sentence from a scrap of paper. He was sweating.

The woman put her cup of tea down on the saucer and just looked at him. She was cool and confident and took her time to reply.

Eventually she said, "pardon?".

He just repeated what was on the piece of paper. The woman, called Sky said,
"OK, Soulmate, tell me about yourself? What's your name?"

The old man whispered, "Wonder".

It was as though he was scared and someone was watching him. Sky picked up her cup and drank some tea whilst scanning the people sat in the restaurant garden. Most of them were couples, however there was a single man in his thirties speaking on his phone.

Sky got up and walked over to the man. She smiled and kissed him on the cheek. Before she walked off, she slipped a keycard into his jacket pocket. The man barely flinched. Sky walked off and returned to her hotel room. She was staying at The Grand Hotel in Brighton and had a beautiful room overlooking the sea. Sky had never stayed there before but unfortunately after today she never would again.

Sky had a unique job whereby she had the ability to stay hidden in full view of the public. She is a lady in her late thirties, average build, conservative clothing and hair and once met, instantly forgotten. There was nothing memorable about her, no tattoos, no scars and had the ability to blend in, she was like an arctic fox, but in the bustling city.

An hour passed and her hotel door was unlocked. The younger gentleman from the restaurant entered. Sky was sat on the sofa with her legs crossed. He had a brown leather bag and walked over to her, he placed the bag on to the coffee table and said nothing. He moved over to the bed and lay down. Sky picked up the bag and left the room, she headed for the foyer where she was hailed a taxi.

Sky worked for the British Intelligence Service MI5. This was called "a drop". A paranoid Russian spy had made contact and was concerned about his country's future. He had good intentions, but if the current regime in Russia were to find out then he would be tried for treason or worse. In the bag was information and a code for a satellite that would give the British access to Russia's next move. Sky was driven to London where she met her superior and handed over the bag.

Sky wasn't a decision maker in the MI5 she was an operative, going from location to location doing various tasks for her country. Sky enjoyed it, there was a sense of danger but there wasn't time to settle down with someone. She enjoyed dressing up and going out with friends, but the older she got the less this happened. Part of her wanted to be normal.

Sky's next mission was to return to Brighton and follow the Russian national who had given her the bag. MI5 just wanted to make sure he wasn't attempting to trick them with a distraction and have them busy looking in one direction when the Russians move in another.

After locating him and tracking his movements for a few days, Sky began to enjoy watching him. He was polite and kind to people, he exercised and was a good-looking guy. Sky began to wear more attractive clothing and would do her hair differently. She was ordered not to make contact but she kinda wanted to.

Sky followed him to the seafront one day whilst he went for a walk but got too close, he recognised her. He hid behind a motor home on Madeira Drive and confronted her as she walked past. Sky denied following him and claimed it was a coincidence. He didn't believe her but after a while he invited her for a drink, his motivation was purely for self preservation.

They had a few drinks and actually got on quite well, Sky found him charming and attractive. His name was Pete, and he seemed like a genuine good person. He told Sky that he had to fly to Budapest the next day, he had some work to do. Sky was smitten and after a passionate kiss he asked her if she would accompany him.

Sky broke protocol and went to Budapest, if her superiors found out she would have been in serious trouble. Pete and Sky had a wonderful time together, they went to the Hungarian National Gallery, the Buda Castle and had long lunches in Heroes' Square. It was romantic and something that had been missing from her life for years. Sky was worried about getting old and being alone but now she had met someone, and she was elated.

On their last day they went to Margaret Island, it was a green oasis on the river Danube. It was beautiful and extremely romantic. Pete whispered into her ear, "I'm your soulmate".
Those words, the words which brought them together a few weeks ago were now repeated but this time they meant the world to Sky.

They traveled back to England together with love in their eyes and an unknown but exciting future to look forward to. Sky had received a message from HQ that she was to abort her mission. MI5 suspected that the Russian intelligence services had discovered a leak which could lead them back to Pete. Sky was ordered not to tell him anything as it would compromise their own operation.

Sky refused to listen and returned to Brighton to warn Pete. Together they could disappear for a year or two and escape this nightmare. When she got back to the hotel, she was informed that Pete was in hospital. Sky panicked but was reassured it was just because he'd sprained his ankle slipping out of the bath.

Sky jumped in a taxi to see the clumsy man; she was going to make fun out of him when she got to the hospital. She got in the lift and walked down the sterile corridor to his room, as she got close a nurse walked past her, she had a face mask on which struck Sky as odd. When she opened the door Pete was fast asleep, Sky put her hand through his hair then sat down. After a few moments she realised Pete was extremely quiet, she got up and tried to wake him, she couldn't. He wouldn't wake. On the floor next to the bed was a used needle, discarded like that first crumpled note which read, "I'm your soulmate".

There was still some liquid left in the needle, Sky was crying, she was heartbroken, she picked it up and said, I wonder.....

The End

Coke and Tears

Welcome to the wonderful world of Edward, or Ed as everyone else apart from his father called him. Ed was a spoilt brat but there was a caring side to him. Born to Lord and Lady Collyer, they lived in a Manor Estate in Dorset. His father was an important man, and his title was the fourth highest in the British peerage system. He spent most of his time at the House of Lords, making money for old rope and socialising in private clubs.

Ed was sent to boarding school like his older brother and sister, it was a beautiful school in the countryside of West Sussex. It became home because Ed only went back to Dorset for the school holidays. It was always nice for Ed to go home but he would often get lonely because his sister and brother were older and didn't want to hang out with him. They had better things to do.

The house was great for hide and seek, there were so many nooks and crannies to get lost in. However, it did get a bit eerie at night with the wind making howling noises down the corridors, on some nights it sounded like a pack of wolves. There were gothic features which fascinated him and the artwork in one particular room had five Doom paintings. These depicted the Last Judgment from God, horrific and gruesome, they were painted to scare people into behaving or going to hell. Ed loved and loathed them depending on his mood. There was a lingering smell in the house he would never forget, it smelt like flowers, lilies maybe.

When Ed was ten his mother passed away. He would never talk about it. It had such a terrible effect on everyone close to her. She was such a kind person, his father met her when she was only eighteen, she had a difficult start to life, but Ed was never privy to the details. Ed's sister, Lily took the tragedy worse than anyone, she went off the rails and disappeared, but that's another story.

The Lord didn't mourn for long and remarried just eighteen months later. Ed found it hard but on the few occasions he met his stepmother she was kind and left him to his own devices. By now Henry, his older brother was twenty-two and after graduating he moved to North London and worked in the city. Ed was surprised and saddened by how easy his father and brother had moved on.

In school, Ed had to share a room with Mason, they got on well and loved sneaking out and exploring the old buildings, looking for underground tunnels and bunkers. The school was called Christ's Hospital, and the students were made to wear long dark blue coats and yellow socks, it was very traditional as these places usually are, it was older than the United States of America. Mason was from Essex, his father was a surgeon, Mason was a bit wild and would smoke cigarettes and weed, he even introduced Ed to cocaine. This was a bad move, Ed loved getting high, it changed him.

School flew by, Ed was obsessed with football, he played and was pretty good, he captained the school team. Life was good, he wanted for nothing, he was even in a band. The problem with having it all on a plate was that Ed and his chums felt superior to others. They would be rude and offensive, maybe a politician in the making. Deep down Ed still wasn't really happy, there was something missing.

Ed became an undergraduate at Exeter University. By now, like many people his age, he started partying hard. Three, four nights a week they were out getting drunk and high, it was chaotic. Ed loved it, he became confident and was able to meet girls, he would be the life and soul, and his exploits became legendary.

Ed had always loved Exeter, and it wasn't too far from his home. Ed joined a band at University called "Butterscotch Envy". They were fairly funky with a great lead singer; Ed was on base guitar. They played at local pubs and clubs and were getting noticed online but it takes a lot of luck to make it big. The posh boys would dress up in secondhand clothes and mess their hair up to try and look working class. They were worried about their privileged lives being exposed and ruining any street cred they had.

Ed liked a drink with his mates and now a few grams of cocaine became the norm. It was like the icing on the cake. The buzz was addictive, Ed became a different person, he felt superhuman when he was high, he floated above the crowd. When Ed wasn't, he was depressed. He had to play a straight bat when he was at home as his father couldn't find out. He even wore long sleeves to hide his self harm cuts. The gravy train would be stopped just like with his sister. By all accounts the heir, Henry was now engaged and doing "super" well. However, poor Lily hadn't ever recovered from losing her mother, and had all but stopped contact with the family. She was supposed to be in the Brighton area, Ed really missed her but she was an adult so had to make her own path, but that didn't stop him worrying about her. When their mother died, Ed would sneak into Lily's bed for comfort, he would never forget that, he loved her. Ed had heard that Lily was on heroin, it broke his heart.

After graduating, Ed stayed in the band, and they organised a UK tour. "Butterscotch Envy" was going all the way up the UK via, Bath, Bristol, Swansea, Cardiff, Manchester, Liverpool and then back down to Coventry, Birmingham, Milton Keynes, London and the final date was to be in Brighton. It was going to be messy. They had a minibus and would stay in cheap hotels.

The tour was a lively affair. Most of the venues were a sellout. The drugs were flowing and a few of the group had a visit from the ambulance service. Stomach pumped, lack of food, sleep deprivation and the lows were so bad that the only way to pick themselves back up was another hit of whizz or coke. They were on the fast track to dependency. They didn't know they were addicts until they nearly died from it. When Ed was using, he didn't care whether he lived or died, he believed it helped him.

The last gig was in Brighton, it was at the Concord Club. As usual the boys went out and performed with vigour and passion, they were still buzzing after the encore. The crowd screamed for more and swayed together like the ocean. Afterwards they went to a house party in a run down house or was it a squat. It was packed full of people drinking, smoking weed and dancing. Ed was on coke as usual and steaming; he went upstairs for a pee, he went into the wrong room and there was a young woman lying face down on the bed.

Ed wanted to wake her to see what she looked like. He prodded her and kept telling her to wake, he went to the bathroom and came back with some water. He was convinced the water would wake her so threw it on her head, nothing!
When he couldn't rouse her, he got his hands under her left shoulder and turned her over, there was blood on her wrist. The young woman's hair was messy and all over her face, Ed moved it to the side and then realised who it was.

Ed froze, this woman wouldn't move, wouldn't wake, this woman was dead. This woman was his missing sister, his beautiful Lily.

Her friends called her Chaos.

The End.

Life Begins at 50

At the age of 50, Mina had a life altering experience. Already a mother of three, and a devoted wife, she now found herself having to come to terms with what had just happened.

She awoke from a long sleep and went to the bathroom; she looked in the mirror and saw the same old Mina staring back, but her life was never going to be the same again.

Mina and her husband, Jake, had a lot to talk about. He had just saved her life, or had he imprisoned her in a world of misery and pain? Should Mina be grateful or disgusted at what Jake had done to her? She was so confused.

After what seemed like days of talking, Jake had opened up on his history; he spoke of his upbringing, his parents, his first kill and his love for his wife and his children. Mina had a million questions but just listened. Jake had a gentle but authoritative way about him and being old fashioned, she loved and obeyed her husband.

They both had the opportunity to live mortal lives, which previously, Jake had vowed to himself that he would do. However, now Mina was embedded into his world, they could choose immortality together. Jake didn't want to live without Mina, but now he didn't have to.

Jake trained his wife, like his parents taught him. A rigorous exercise which ensured Mina was able to learn all there was to know about being a creature of the night, a blood sucking moroaica. It went against Mina's good nature, but she could feel herself changing. Her desires had changed and her thirst for fresh blood was an itch that needed scratching.

Her first kill was moments away, she was nervous. Mina had crept into an orphanage; it was late and children were asleep. She floated past their beds, careful not to step on any noisy floorboards. She didn't want to wake the precious children; she wanted her kill to be silent.

Jake had done his homework on the orphanage and discovered that Nun Lessa had a
reputation for torturing the poor parentless little ones. She would throw their food on the floor, beat them and make their lives a miserable nightmare. She was perfect for the taking, nobody would miss her.

As Jake had taught her, she used chloroform to make sure Nun Lessa was unconscious, she then made an incision with a razor blade and drank the fresh metallic liquid for one minute. Enough for a meal but not enough to leave a suspicious scene. The razor blade was left and the (forced) suicide was complete. Mina was a natural, it made her feel alive, completely invincible.

Her second kill didn't run like clockwork. Firstly, the target had miraculously died all on their own; they had a heart attack. The third kill went well, or so she thought. Her intended target had been drinking alcohol all day, and as a non-drinking person, Mina felt the effects on her way home and almost got lost. Each feed was a learning curve and she eventually perfected it.

If it could be possible, the marriage was even stronger and Jake no longer had to operate behind Mina's back, or so he thought he was. They could be honest and were able to talk about every single thing.

At Mina's reawakening when Jake brought her into this world, she announced the words.
"I knew, I always knew you fool".

The late-night disappearing acts from Jake were poorly executed, and the blood splatter on his clothing was enough to make this loyal wife question his motives. After a while the cunning Mina was able to link together her husband's movements with a string of suicides in the region.

Was she shocked?
Of course she was, but after she researched the history of the region with the help of an old man at the library, she understood. The old stranger knew a lot about the night walker's. Mina didn't have any hard evidence but had strong suspicions he was a vampire.

Mina became ambitious; much more ambitious than Jake and wanted to rebuild the castle that belonged to her husband's family in Hunedoara, a city in the region of Transylvania. Jake was convinced by Mina, and they organised the construction of his ancestral home.

The castle was originally built in the 15th century by a Prince called Vlad III, also known as Vlad the Impaler, also known as Vlad Dracula. Famed for dipping his bread into the blood of his impaled victims.

It took four years of hard work before this historical piece of architecture was finally completed. Jake and Mina Dracul moved into their new abode. They were now Lord and Lady of Hunedoara. They took their rightful title and were treated like royalty, but they were concerned of how their flamboyant lifestyle looked.

Spending years in various parts of Europe was the only way they could continue their lifestyle and not draw attention to their gruesome lifestyle. They had houses in Prague, Budapest, London and Paris, but their home was always in Transylvania.

Everything was perfect until Michel their son knocked on their door.....

Michel had followed in his parent's footsteps; however he was less successful and less subtle. Michel had moved to Finland; he liked the cold weather but there was something he enjoyed more.

Notoriety.

Michel loved the attention his moniker was receiving but he took it too far. He was called the "Perkele", which means "evil spirit', in Finnish. Michel had developed a taste for the nobility. He claimed their blood tasted sweeter.

After years of picking off hundreds of the aristocracy and becoming a folk law horror story to the local children, the powers to be suspected the flamboyant Michel was to blame. He denied any wrongdoing; however he was run out of the country. So naturally, he ran home to his parents.

Finnish headhunters followed Michel to Romania. This was incredibly bad news for subtle and generous Jake and Mina, they now found themselves in the firing line. They reprimanded their son but couldn't give him up to the authorities. They had to protect their son at any cost.

The friendly old man from the library all of those years ago came to see the family at their castle. He introduced himself as "The Fly Man", also known as Renfield. He explained that for many years he had served the family. For the last century he was just watching from afar, but now he sensed their perilous position.

They hatched a plan to leave the country and disappear for many years by travelling through Russia. In such a huge country, they would be able to hide in plain sight. The date was set and Renfield was going to stay and look after the castle.

Unfortunately, before they could leave, the castle was surrounded by law enforcement and locals. They wanted revenge and wanted to destroy the castle and everything in it.

The first thing they did was smash the windows and threw petrol bombs in. The smoke pushed the family upstairs as the mob was attempting to force the huge front door. The fire gained traction and began spreading like a pandemic. Parts of the castle began collapsing and the family began to panic. They attempted to fly away but the smoke made it impossible. There was only one place to go.

They fought their way through the fire into the basement, where they had a crypt. They bundled themselves in just as the castle completely collapsed like a pack of cards. They were buried under hundreds of tons of rubble and debris. Escape looked impossible.

The mob searched for the family's carcasses to no avail. The locals believed the whole family had perished so they fled the scene. The Dracul family became a myth, a legend to the rest of Europe. A scary story for a scout leader to tell around the campfire.

One morning a scout leader went to have a shave but couldn't because his razor blade had vanished.....

The End

Lord Have Mercy

Six in the morning, Police are at the door. Philippa
answered it with a dressing gown draped over herself.
"What is it?" She barked.
"Madam, can we come in, we need to talk to you and your
husband?"

Philippa let the two male officers in, one was very young, and the other was in his forties, looking like he'd had a long night. She showed them to the living room and went upstairs to wake her husband.

Rewind many years.....

Lord and Lady Collyer were products of the UK aristocracy. Born to the manor, some would say they had won the lottery. Inheriting titles, money, land and a beautiful country mansion. Surely this is everyone's dream.

A dream, however in reality it was a nightmare.

The Lord had always lived in this mansion, other than when he was at boarding school. The house was huge and as a child he loved to investigate, searching around the grounds looking for anything exciting. One day when he was eight, he found the basement, it was dusty and damp and smelt a bit stale. Under some plastic coverings were some large picture's. They were really odd and quite scary, they had figures that looked like they were being tortured and in pain. This intrigued him and he spent ages just staring at them. He couldn't believe someone might have to go through all of that pain.

When he was twenty his parents went to mainland Europe for a break, but unfortunately, they never made it back. It was 1987 and they were travelling back to the UK on a car ferry. As it left the port of Zeebrugge in Belgium the ferry capsized, the bow doors were left open which allowed water onboard. 193 people died that day including his parents.

Overnight he took his father's title and became Lord Collyer, he was now a Viscount. He was extremely young to take this responsibility but that was the life they led.

Let's not forget about the death of his parents, he was now an orphan. He got on fairly well with them, he was closer to his father. They used to walk and climb together in the Lake District. Those trips were some of the best times he'd ever had.
His father was a very traditional man and at times their relationship was formal, but not of the trips to Cumbria.

After a few years of cosplaying as a Viscount, he needed a wife, someone to live and share this life with him. He was set up with various "rich little princesses"but couldn't take their entitled behaviour. He was too impatient and wanted a nice humble girl. He took a fancy to a petite cleaner at his house. She was a brunette, thin, blue eyes and had a few tattoos that he noticed. Was it lust or love.

The Lord took a chance, and they got closer and closer. It was love; however his peers didn't agree as she wasn't from their background, she was a commoner. Her name was Emma (yes, different to the lady at the start of the story).

Dressed up, Emma looked every bit a lady, she looked elegant, some said she resembled Audrey Hepburn. However, under the surface was a young girl with a history of crime and drug abuse. Emma hid it from her new husband, he was naïve when it came to the streets. He had been protected his whole life. Maybe the mystery was part of the attraction.

Together the Lord and Lady had three children, Henry, Lily and Edward. The children were farmed off to boarding schools and Emma got lonely. When an ex-drug addict becomes bored, they tend to go back to what they know. She was rattling around in an huge house with nothing to do. Emma went back to using heroin, it was easy. The Lord was always away on business and she didn't have to break the law anymore because she had money.

Some people are able to use heroin and continue a relatively normal life, it's called being a high functioning addict. She would smoke it, so she didn't leave any track marks on her arms. They were so ugly and looked a pin cushion. Emma loved using, she would sleep for days on end, it was as though she was in hibernation. She was taken away from any pain and memories of her difficult upbringing. Emma had been burying these memories for years. She was abused by her uncle, but that a different story.

One morning the Lord left for London, Emma called her dealer to drop some drugs off. Dave the dealer knocked at the door, as she opened it two masked men rushed her, she fought back and in the fracas, she smashed her head on the marble floor. She died. Blood spilled out covering the marble, it was a horrendous scene. The perpetrators panicked and left in a rush before they could steal anything. They were never caught.

A 10-year-old boy, a 13 year old girl and the oldest and heir, Henry were left without a mother. The Lord was devastated, his wife had been taken in such awful circumstances. She was so kind and gentle. It shocked her husband when he finally found out about her drug use. After the post mortem the toxicologist report showed that Emma had Opiates in her blood. The Lord was distraught and turned to the deadly drink, it took him a while to get back on his feet, and when he did he met Philippa.

Philippa was a divorcee and was friends with a colleague. She was charming and pretty and would fit the title of Lady. The wedding was a success but was missing one person. His daughter, Lily.

Lily had been off the grid for a few years. She'd attended the University of Brighton but after that she stopped all contact. The Lord had paid Private Detectives to find her, but they never did. The last he'd heard was that she was a drug user, like her mother. The apple doesn't fall far from the tree. The two boys seemed to be doing well, Henry was working in the city and Edward was in a band.

Back to the six o'clock police knock...

The Lord and Lady sat there, nervous and dreading the news that was just about to spill out of these public servants' mouths.

"I'm sorry to have to tell you this but we've found your daughter Lily. We found her dead at a house in Brighton. It appears she has died from an overdose. Your son Edward was also at the house, and he's been arrested for supplying the illegal drugs that caused her death".

The Lord fell back on to the sofa and his wife hugged him. He couldn't move; he was paralysed from the neck down. Was he going to lose two children in one night? One to the heavens and one to prison.

The police continued, "When we got to the house, Edward was hysterical and was screaming one word over and over again".

"What was it officer?"

He just kept screaming, "Cas or Caosh, we couldn't tell, he was in a trance!"

The Lord moved his head to face the officers and said,

"It was Chaos, he was saying Chaos, my beautiful daughter was known as Chaos!"

The End.

<u>The Letter</u>

Great News, or at least it was meant to be.

Ben was working in a warehouse; it was hard work but good fun. Today though, was a big day, possibly a life changing day. Ben was so nervous and unable to concentrate on anything he was doing at work.

Mike, a colleague of his knew something was up. At lunchtime he told Ben to drive home and check the mail. It was only a ten-minute drive but it felt like Ben was driving to the moon. He pulled up on his parent's driveway and through the porch glass door he could see the post.

All scattered on the floor like it was trying to look for hiding places. Ben unlocked the door and found the white A4 envelope addressed to him. As he picked it up it felt heavy, not like a single letter but a bundle of information which would hopefully take him on to the next level of his life.

Ben's hands were shaking as he tore at the envelope like a kid on Christmas Day. The first word his eyes were homed in on like a laser beam was "Congratulations".

Oh boy, what had he done, he thought. Ben knew life was going to change, including his old buddies. Some wouldn't like it but it was his life and his future, and he had to do what was right for him.

At the tender age of twenty-two Ben had joined the ranks of the police. He was going to be a Police Constable. There was a lot of training and studying to do to get Ben past his probationary period, but he was excited.

Ben was still shaking with adrenaline whilst skimming through the paperwork. There was a date on his joining instructions, and it was a mere six weeks away.
After work Ben drove home to share the news with his family, they were excited, and his younger sister hugged him. Izzy was asking all sorts of questions, most of them Ben couldn't answer because he just didn't know. All he knew was he had to be at the police HQ on 30th October. Later on that day, Ben told his girlfriend Ellie the news. He'd only been seeing Ellie for a few months and she was worried about Ben leaving. She was concerned he might meet someone else. Ellie was sweet but a bit clingy. Ben met Ellie in a nightclub after he saved her from some aggressive guy who was shouting and screaming at her.

Time flew and but Ben still had time to contemplate whether he should go forward with this appointment. He spoke with friends and family and after a while decided that he may as well give it a go as it's not like the army, you can leave whenever you want.

The 30th came and Ben had packed a bag to last him five days, this was going to be nerve racking for him. On arrival Ben was given a key to a room and told to drop his things off. The room was small, had a single bed, wardrobe and a sink. It was soulless, there were no pictures, no TV and

Ben had to share a bathroom, he just hoped it wasn't with a bunch of slobs.

Ben went to the meeting point upstairs and met with other new recruits. Fortunately Ben is quite likeable, so he met a few guys that were of a similar age and they seemed good fun. They discussed their concerns and where they were from. They got on well and decided pretty quickly to go for a drink after the first session had finished. The guys met up later and had a laugh together and Ben soon forgot about his anxiety and began to relax. Ben settled in and cracked on with his training.

Ben got arrested.

He was four days into his training, it was Friday, Ben was looking forward to going home and seeing friends and family.

Was it over before it started?

Ben was asleep in his single bed, in his single room at HQ. Whilst stirring, he heard the lock of his door being fiddled with, before he could fully grasp what was happening, his door flew open.
Six police officers came in, two jumped on him and handcuffed Ben to his rear. One officer arrested Ben, but Ben was so shocked he couldn't take it in. He was helped up, searched and whipped away to custody.

It all happened so quickly; it wasn't until they got to the custody desk that he realised that he was arrested for murder. Ben almost fainted. He couldn't believe it, before he knew it, he was in a cell, with the cell door slammed shut with a horrible noise he would never forget, it was like an anvil being dropped on his head, Bang! The police were searching his room and examining his phone, whilst Ben was shell shocked in a tiny cell with an uncomfortable bed. It smelt of disinfectant and he was thinking about all of the other people that had been held in there.

The cell door slowly opened; it was the custody sergeant. He was calm and professional, he's not part of the investigation, so he was just there to make sure Ben was ok and told him that Ellie was dead. He could only give brief details, but Ellie had been killed in the local town.

Ben couldn't figure out why Ellie was even there, she lived eighty miles away. After several hours, Ben was able to speak to a solicitor. Anne, the solicitor explained the situation and Ellie was stabbed behind the high street in an alleyway. They pieced together that Ellie had followed him to the area, probably because she lacked trust in him. She was found by a drunken couple on their way home, but it was too late for her, she'd bled to death.

Ben was devastated for Ellie, but couldn't understand why he had been arrested, he had witnesses. He was in the gym at HQ with five others. After his interview with two veteran detectives, he was finally released. They didn't have enough to charge and remand him, so he was bailed with conditions.

Ben went home, completely exhausted, emotionally drained and didn't know what to do with himself. He eventually slept, and he slept for a long, long time. His future was in the balance.

Ben just existed for a few months in a state of depression, loss and anxiety. He couldn't go back to training after his arrest, he would forever have a cloud over his head. When he spoke to Anne, the solicitor just before he had to return on bail, she explained that Ellie had been following him, but she too was being stalked by her ex boyfriend, the guy from the nightclub.

Police had arrested him, after CCTV was found. Ben was relieved but left his parent's house to get some space. Whilst driving to the Lake District, he was involved in a car crash. A silver Ford Focus came out of nowhere and had a head on collision with Ben. It was catastrophic, an air ambulance came and took Ben to hospital. It was too late and Ben died, he was hit by an unmarked police vehicle.

The End.

The Morning After.

Imagine waking up in a police cell. Confused, cold, hurting and suffering from withdrawal. Ed didn't believe he was an addict until he almost died from it.

Ed was wearing a terrible blue paper body suit that the police give you when they've seized all of your clothes, it makes a scratching sound when it's moved. The cell was tiny, painted concrete, cold to the touch, the windows were just cloudy thick glass bricks. It was like being buried alive, the bed was a hard plastic mattress with one thin blanket, he could have been anywhere, Siberia, Iceland but probably Brighton. The view was bleak, similar to his future.

Ed had a sip of water from his plastic cup and tried to focus. What on earth had happened? Why the hell had he been arrested?

"Focus Ed, focus, concentrate, what happened?" Ed said out loud.

There was a pain in his stomach, it was horrible, a knot just eating away inside. It affected his mind, his appetite and his confidence. It was the dreaded anxiety. An underrated feeling that had been overlooked on the torture scene. Im sure Mad Frankie Fraser could have attempted the anxiety root instead of electric shocking his victims' testicles.

Anxiety, a drinker's companion. A pain in the form of madness. It makes you ill and the only substance that can make it go away and put you back on top is more booze.

The first drink is disgusting and will probably make a person sick. You look at yourself in the mirror and think why am I doing this? You pour a second glass, this is better. It goes down smoothly, now you're flying. You can do anything, other than balance properly. You wobble rather than walk, you think you're getting away with it, but you're not.

Add drug withdrawal on top and you are having the worst morning of your life. Especially now you're stuck in a locked cold cell. You can't tell anyone, because everyone judges, and you've admitted your addiction. A man can't do that, it's weak and pathetic. There's now only one way out.

How do you do it in a cell? There's nothing sharp, no noxious chemicals to swig or nothing to tie around your throat. The CCTV camera is watching. Big brother is peering at your every move. The desire to fall asleep and never wake up is so appealing. The amount of times Ed has previously woken up and was disappointed. "Great! Another day to get through. Maybe I won't wake up tomorrow morning".

This was an everyday experience for Ed, but when you're in a band you can do it, in fact it's expected. So here Ed was. He remembered that his sister had died. "Poor Lily "he thought.

Bang, then clunk as the cell door was opened. It flew open to a middle-aged man stood at the doorway. Ed didn't know what to say, but the man, a custody sergeant asked him if he was ok and if he wanted anything. Ed's head felt it was being pinged around a pinball machine. Ed thought a pint of vodka was probably out of the question, so he asked for a tea.

An Englishman's answer to all of our problems. There's a perfect temperature to drink a cup of tea. Too hot and you're scolding your mouth, the skin will come off. If you leave it too long it turns lukewarm, not great. But every now and then you can catch it just right and it becomes the best drink in the world. Comforting, tasty, refreshing pure nectar to the addict.

The Custody Sergeant told Ed that he would be interviewed in a couple of hours, but before that he could speak to the duty solicitor. Ed was really concerned he was going to be sent to prison, even though he knew he hadn't done anything wrong. He found his sister dead; he didn't kill her.

After explaining everything to the solicitor, Ed was shown into an interview room and as advised he simply told the truth. He'd finished a gig and went to an after party. Ed went upstairs and found a girl lying face down on a bed. He turned her over and it was his lovely older sister, she had overdosed and had died.

The enquiries were long and complicated for the police, such as speaking to witnesses, finding out who supplied the drugs and the timings of his movements. The police had to release Ed under strict bail conditions as they didn't have enough evidence to charge him.

All Ed thought about was buying a bottle of vodka as soon as he got out of there. He checked into a hotel and drank for three days straight. The effects of drinking, passing out, drinking, passing out had a hallucinogenic effect on him. Ed was tripping, what was a dream and what was reality?

Knock, knock, knock. Ed thought it was the chambermaid, but no it was Rob and Sid, two of his band mates from Butterscotch Envy. They had found him after two days of looking in drug dens and hotels. They drove him to Dorset and dropped him at his father's country house. Ed's father was a big deal and was a Viscount. Remnants of old England and their hereditary titles. Ed had an older brother, so it was unlikely he was going to become a Lord.

Ed's father and stepmother looked after him in their odd formal manner, but he thought it was kind of them, considering his father had just lost his daughter. However, Ed struggled, he couldn't get to a shop and his father hid all of the booze. Long nights, the shakes and the sweats were terrible. Somehow, he got through the first week and was feeling a little better, but a long way off from perfect.

Ed began to write music again, like he did when he was a teenager. It killed the time and was productive to a point. His sister's funeral was an extremely difficult time for Ed and his family. It was too much for Ed, there were a lot of people there and a beautiful arrangement of the word "Chaos" written in flowers. His sister's nickname.

When everyone had gone to bed, Ed went looking for the alcohol, it was a huge house so there were many rooms to check. After an hour of searching, he came across a locked door in the cellar. He'd never noticed it before but thought it had probably been locked for years. The next day, he went back to the cellar when his father was out as he was intrigued by this secretive door, was the alcohol stashed away in it?

Ed brought some spare keys down that he had found in a drawer in the dining room. He tried each key, but none seemed to work. Whilst he was about to leave there was a scratching noise coming from the room. It was faint but he'd definitely heard something, was it a rat or a squirrel? Ed called out but there was no response, so he gave up and went back to his room.

A few days went past, and curiosity got the better of Ed so he went back down to see if he could pick the lock with some metal scraps he had found. That didn't work either but this time he could hear a dragging noise. It was like there was a sack of coal being dragged along the floor inside this locked room. Ed called out, "hello", but nothing, then more scratching. Ed had to find out what was going on, he went upstairs and spoke with his stepmother, Philippa. She was completely dumbfounded, she had no idea what he was talking about but went down to the cellar with him to check it out. At first there was nothing but after they knocked on the door there was a sound. It sounded like a cough and some weak knocking. It couldn't be an animal, its noises were too human.

They couldn't ignore this and went and got the gardener, Simon who brought some tools with him. It took a while, but he eventually got the door wedged open. Ed was the first to look, it was dark, it smelt of stale eggs and there were bags and blankets on the floor. He then noticed a silhouette to the left in the back. There was a shape, it moved but didn't speak, it looked human.

They pulled the door open and shone a torch in, they were all a bit scared as it was the unknown, it was so odd. Ed was shaking. The torch light made the figure hide behind a blanket to protect its eyes. They walked into the room, "hello, can you hear me?". There was no reply to Ed's question, they moved closer and they discovered it was a woman. There was a woman locked up in their cellar. They couldn't believe it, had Ed's father been keeping this terrible secret? How long had this poor person been kept there?

They walked the woman out and took her to the kitchen where there was a warm fire and some tea being made. The woman was disheveled, her hair was wild and knotted, her clothes were filthy, she was probably in her fifties. They did their best to clean her and help but the woman was scared and didn't know what was happening.

Suddenly the father had come home, they could hear him walking towards the kitchen. The woman began to panic, and they had to hold her down. The father walked in and almost fainted, he couldn't believe it, he didn't know what to say, they had found his guilty secret.

After a lot of shouting and crying they eventually got the truth out of the Viscount. The person who was locked up in a room in the cellar, was the Viscounts first wife, or as he described her as his "mad wife". The woman who was supposed to be dead. Ed believed that she died when he was ten, but here she was. The Viscount had kept her locked up for ten years. It was Ed's real mother. He cried uncontrollably, the feelings of happiness and sadness collided in his head. He felt like his head was in a vice.

It was crazy. Many normal families would have called the police, but Ed had a deep mistrust of the police, so they forced the Viscount into the room in which his mother was held and secured the door.
He kept shouting, "she's crazy, I had to do it, I thought she was going to kill the children".

They needed time to figure out their next move. Ed's stepmother took the poor mumbling lady upstairs to clean her and get her some fresh clothes. She needed her dignity back.

Little did they know that Simon the gardener had called the police behind their backs, he didn't feel comfortable with the situation. The police showed up en masse within minutes, they whisked the Viscount off in handcuffs and two policewomen stayed at the house to interview Ed's real mother. It was a surreal experience.

Ed lay down on his bed in disbelief of the carnage which had taken place.

It was simply Chaos.

The End

Tom The Vampire

Growing up in a Sussex village Tom loved life. He played for the local football team, went to a decent school and had a number of great friends. They were really close and loved winding each other up. Life was good. Tom was 16 and in Year 11, he was only a few months away from his GCSE exams, but was confident he would do well.

Tom was an athletic boy, he could run fast, think fast and jump extremely high. He lived with his parents; they were kind and supportive. Tom was an only child and never felt he really fitted in with the extended family. He had a pale complexion and was six foot tall. His parents were different, short, stout and had a darker skin tone, Tom towered over them.

Out of the blue, Tom received an email which stated in the subject line; "There's something you should know". Immediately, he thought it was Spam so ignored it. A week went past, and he received another email. Then a week later, another. It was annoying but Tom gave in out of curiosity and opened the message. It read,

"All is not what it seems. You will be changing soon, and you'll need to adapt. The only way for you to survive is if you meet with us.
We can help you. Please reply.
Your Mother and Father."

Tom immediately thought it was a wind up, maybe one of his mates was playing a joke on him. However, for a laugh, Tom replied,
"Hi Mother and Father, I can meet with you, somewhere public. When and where?"

A reply, simply said,
"Great, Ichor Coffee Bar, 11am tomorrow".

That was it, Tom thought that this could be a laugh, and he wondered what his friends would do when he actually showed up.

He'd never been to Ichor Coffee Bar before but knew where it was. It always looked dark and mysterious, so Tom was intrigued.

Tom woke up at 10:30 the next day and after slowly getting ready he was running late, typical for a 16-year-old. He plodded to the cafe and looked through the window as he arrived, like a secret agent checking out the ground. There were no customers, just a couple of staff. No sign of his friends, he thought that they might be running late so he entered.

It was eerie and had a chill to it. The cafe was dark inside with old dusty paintings on the walls. There was a strange damp smell which was unpleasant and music coming from a speaker on the wall. It was playing some type of foreign music, whilst Tom was sat down waiting, he used Shazam to identify it, as it was odd, but he liked it. It was a Hungarian band called, Omega and the song was gyöngyhajú lány, translated as "The girl with pearls in her hair". Tom found it mesmerising.

Whilst sat in an almost hypnotic and relaxed state, Tom was approached. The middle-aged lady asked him what he would like, she had a strong Eastern European accent. Tom ordered a hot chocolate, it had been his favourite drink since he was a small child and it was like a comfort blanket to him, especially when he felt nervous.

Five minutes later and Tom was still the only person in the cafe. The lady brought his drink over and sat down opposite him, the man at the counter, slowly made his way over without making a sound, almost floating.

The lady said, "Hello Tom, there's no easy way to say this, but I'm your mother and this is your father".
Tom replied, "What are you talking about? I have a mum and dad, who are you?"

The lady explained that they had to give Tom up when he was a newborn. They were not in a position to care for him and that his mum and dad aren't his biological parents. They had to return to Europe as they had a lifestyle which wasn't suitable for a child. Tom listened and listened and was confused but engrossed in her ability to articulate herself. She was wise and thought provoking and led him into a mysterious world.

Tom must have been there for a while, and to cut a long story short, he was told he was going to turn into a bloody vampire. Tom was really hoping this was a joke but, he was informed that he was immortal, which grabbed his attention.
"So, I can't die?" The lady replied, "No, but there are ways you could be murdered, have you heard of a stake through the heart?"

Tom realised that immortality was sustainable but with conditions; main condition, don't annoy people who might want to kill you!

They claimed they were originally from Budapest, but due to their lifestyles they have had to move around the continent. Being vampires themselves, they had to be careful not to draw too much attention.

Tom wanted to know how his life would change, what was going to happen to his body, would sunlight damage him? So many questions went through his dizzy mind. He felt like he was in some surreal movie.

Another hot chocolate was brought over to him. He sat quietly for a while and looked around. The cafe was really run down, and the pictures were all faded. He wondered why the adults kept looking out of the window and why they kept disappearing into the back room.

Then suddenly, behind him he could hear the front door open. Footsteps behind him and a muffled noise. Probably more customers, he thought. Tom slowly turned around and it was his friends laughing their heads off, giving him a push saying, "Got Ya".

Tom, at this point realised he was part of an elaborate joke, and he was the main target.
"You bastards", Tom said, over and over. He eventually joined in the laughter. His "new mother and father

"appeared behind the counter and apologised whilst laughing. They had just bought the cafe and they all thought they could have some fun before it was renovated. Tom was an easy target as he was always talking about why he looked so different to his family.

Tom eventually went home, feeling like an idiot. This was going to follow him around for ever.

Tom was no longer a vampire!

The End

Emma's Nightmare.

Emma grew up with an alcoholic father and a mother who had little time for her. They lived in a three-bedroom council house in Wareham, Dorset. It was dull and boring, and she felt like life was passing her by, no boyfriend, no prospects and no hope. The biggest employer in the town was the local hospital.

Emma got little out of school and hung around with local friends that would rather hang around the streets than go home. Smoking and drinking was something they all did and every now and then they would do some shoplifting, just for sweets and drinks. Unfortunately, this led to more boredom and some of the boys upped their risk taking. It started with cannabis and eventually she was introduced to smoking heroin. It was a habit she had for a while, but fortunately, she never became dependent on it.

Emma's mother was a part time cleaner at the hospital and with Emma's lack of qualifications she managed to get Emma a casual job there. It was something to do and gave her some money, but she didn't like it, who would?

Emma used to watch the busy nurses rushing around taking care of patients and wondered if she would ever be able to do it. She once mentioned it to her father, looking for some encouragement and motivation but it never came.

He just laughed at Emma and said,
"They'd never hire someone like you, girls like you are only good for cleaning".

Whilst at the hospital, and becoming depressed, she made friends with a few of the girls. They used to go out every now and then, nothing special, just the cinema or the pub. After several months, one of the girls told Emma that she was leaving, she heard there was a cleaning job at a local country house. The money was better than the NHS so Emma begged her friend to let her join with her.

The country house was amazing, with beautiful grounds and a huge fountain. It was huge but there was only one man living there. He was in his twenties and was recently made into a Viscount after his parents died. He wasn't around very often but when he was, he had to be addressed as "Lord".

Even though there was only one person living at the house there was always plenty to do, each room had antiques and large paintings which collected dust like a castle and the chandeliers were a challenge to clean.

Overtime, Emma saw more and more of the Lord. She felt he was deliberately running into her and making awkward small talk. Emma was shy but she quite liked the attention and had never spoken to someone with a posh accent before. She tried to adapt her accent, so she sounded less common, Emma was embarrassed by her meagre means.

Eventually the Lord made his move and asked Emma to dinner, she was wined and dined and made to feel special. She was a rough diamond that needed some polishing. It was different to the lads from the estate she used to hang around with. They were streetwise and swore in every sentence they spat out. The Lord on the other hand was a class act, handsome, polite, well educated and extremely well dressed. It was two worlds colliding.

Within a month, after a whirlwind of a romance, Emma had moved into the house.
The Lord told her,
"You are the only thing, in any room you're ever in. You'll never find a man that needs you more than I".
He had ways of using words that were as beautiful as a cloud of starlings.

They threw a wonderful party so she could meet his friends and family. It was an incredible night, the ball gowns, the dancing and the gentleman in their tuxedos. It was a fairytale for Emma, it was like she was dreaming, but she knew that one wrong move and she would embarrass him.

Six months later they got married at Sherborne Abbey, a beautiful place founded in 705AD. They honeymooned in Barbados and were waited on hand and foot. It was so relaxing. The reggae music, the rum and the friendly atmosphere was just perfect. Unfortunately, when they got home the Lord had commitments he had to attend, and a large part of his business was in London. They were in love but it hurt Emma when they were apart. It's a big house to be lonely in.

The Lord was spending more and more time away in London with his business dealings and had an apartment in North London. Emma looked like she had it all but what did she have? She had little contact with her family, her friends had their own families and her husband's friends only made contact when they met as couples.

Emma eventually fell into her old ways and began drinking, which got earlier and earlier. This eventually made her feel ill, so she swapped alcohol for heroin. A drug she loved. It took her away into another world, a comforting place where she felt happy. It was a comfort blanket which wrapped around her and kept her safe.

A year later, Emma was pregnant, within five years she had three children. This kept her busy and she hired a live-in nanny to help, her name was Lucy. Not only was this a great help that shared the workload it also gave Emma a companion. The Lord was home every weekend but during the week Emma and the nanny were together raising two boys and a girl.

When the children were old enough, they were sent to boarding school in Horsham, Christ's Hospital. Lucy was no longer needed and quickly found another job. This hit Emma hard, she was alone again, and it felt like a breakup. She was hurting like a lost teenager and to kill the loneliness went back to what she knows, heroin.

Over the coming years, the Lord and Emma grew apart, time alone is not a friend to a relationship. Many emotions become explosive, jealousy, bitterness, depression and anger. This was the relationship killer. The arguments became more intense and frequent and eventually became physical.
Emma was the physical one, she would blow up like a volcano and throw crockery and glasses at the Lord, she would threaten him. Her rough upbringing began to filter through her well worked elegant facade. One night before the children were due back for the summer holidays, she made a threat she would live to regret.

"If I can't have the children, then I may as well kill them. I'll grab a shot gun and shoot them in front of you".

The Lord was shocked and scared for his children's safety, he lost it. During the heat of the argument, he ran after her and chased her into the basement. She panicked and ran into a small room. The Lord caught up with her and stood at the doorway and just stared at her. He didn't know what to do, so he simply shut the door and locked it. He needed time to think.

That was her home for the next ten years. The Lord had made a terrible error and the longer he left it the worse it became. Days became weeks, weeks became months and then it became years. The Lord had to make up an elaborate story and told everyone that she had died. People believed him because of who he was, and the family doctor was open to bribes. For several thousand pounds he signed a death certificate, it was all too easy.

The Lord eventually moved on and remarried a lovely woman called Philippa. Philippa didn't have any idea of the torment another woman was suffering just metres away. She carried on where Emma had left from.

The children took the news of their mother's death badly. Each child suffered in their own way. Self-harm, depression and drugs were part of their journey. Poor Lily, she was only thirteen, her life became a tornado and would end tragically, in Chaos.

The End

The Exploration

It was filthy in there, absolutely disgusting. The smell was horrendous, it was like death, like bodies rotting and falling away. Every sense Rob had was under attack apart from his hearing. It was deathly silent, not a peep from anywhere. Rob contemplated giving up and questioned his life choices.

When he was sixteen, Rob did A-Levels. Classical Civilisation, Economics and English were his choice, twenty years later he still has no idea why he chose them. Then he went to the University of Brighton and completed a degree in Hospitality
Management. Without getting into Rob's love life, which was unusual, these are just some examples of how Rob

lives his life. He may as well throw a dart at a board for his illogical thinking.

Back to the horror, oh the bloody horror. Rob found himself in this situation where he it was so bad he actually thought it was funny. Luckily, he had a hanky is his pocket which was clean enough and he held it up to his nose and mouth to disguise the rancid smell. The place was a cave, a cave in Peru, South America. Rob had just left his career as a tree surgeon, it was a hard tough job with many muscle and joint injuries. He was still strong, but just in short bursts. Peru was somewhere he was interested in due to the Inca's. The human sacrificing, fortress building, civilisation from the 13th century.

Rob and his patient wife, Eve, decided to take this extended vacation as they needed time alone and wanted some adventure. Things were tough between the two and they were hoping this break would help. Little did they know what was going to happen.

Whilst on a guided walking tour through the jungle in search of a pukara (fortress), they noticed a puma was stalking them. During the brief panic, one of the party disappeared, Eve was first to notice. There was only ten of them so it was quite obvious. Especially as it was Zak, a loud, brash and tall American. He was accompanied by his daughter who was around twenty. She was beautiful, sweet and carried herself with class, her name was Helen.

Rob had nicknamed her Helen of Troy which suited her well.

The group spent some time calling out his name and looking around the jungle but to no avail. It was as though he had just vanished into the hue. Helen was beside herself and didn't know what to do, Eve and a few of the ladies in the group were comforting her and trying to reassure her.
As time was ticking by and the sun was setting it was time to find shelter. The jungle is a scary place in the dark with the deadly bugs, snakes and spiders. The group leader made the tough decision to trek to the nearest hut, in Scotland they call them a bothy. It was just big enough for the remaining nine to get comfortable and eat some food. The noises outside were spectacular, it was surreal with rustling, scratching, animals calling and the odd squeal. The mood inside the hut was low with poor Helen imagining the worst for her father.

As the group awoke to the morning bird song, the sun was beginning to rise. It was a beautiful place if it hadn't been for the mysterious disappearance. The group gathered and came up with a plan of action, Rob was trying to be positive and was doing his best to get the group onboard. The group found the area from last night and fanned out searching once again. A few hours went by and as the group were drifting back to the RV point, Eve told of a hole she had found. She couldn't say too much about it, as she hadn't ventured down there as it was dark and scary. Peru is known for its cave systems, so it wasn't a huge surprise, but it had given the group hope.

Eve led the group to the opening, and they gathered around removing the debris from the area to make it more visible. Helen shouted into the hole to see if her father might reply, unfortunately he didn't. The group hatched a plan with their kit and tools that one of their members should get lowered into it to have a look around for any signs of Zak.
Rob was the man. His age, athleticism, size and overall enthusiasm made Rob the obvious choice. If Zak had been there, no doubt he would've put himself above Rob. Rob got kitted up with torches, an axe, compass and obviously a hefty rope to lower and hopefully haul him back up.

Just before Rob went down into the abyss, he received a huge hug from Helen. Rob enjoyed the hug but tried to hide it from his wife. Rob began to get lowered into the darkness, the first thing he noticed was the smell. If you were thrown into a barrel of dead fish then this would be close to the smell. Rob's eyes were beginning to water, his nostrils were swelling up and his head began to ache, in fact it was throbbing.

Down and down Rob went, the rope began to dig into his torso. He turned on a torch to have a better look at what he was up against. It was horrible down there, weeds had managed to grow, roots were coming down from above and the floor was all damp and boggy. Once fully descended he unstrapped the rope and shouted up to his fellow hikers that he was going to investigate. First of all, he looked down to see if there was any obvious landing points where Zak had fallen in, but alas no.

Rob shouted out to Zak, with the hope of a sign of life but nothing. Off his trudged through the boggy floor which squelched as each boot hit the ground. Squelch, squelch, squelch was hard work to walk in, at times it felt like quicksand, it was energy draining. As Rob made his way he could see smaller holes through the cave walls which were too small for a human, but he expected there were plenty of creepy creatures down there.

As Rob made it through a small opening it then hit him what the smell was. Thousands and thousands of bats hanging upside down sleeping. What an odd and petrifying sight, underneath them was tons and tons of guava, stinking, dark coloured bat excrement. It looked like it was moving but it was just various cockroaches and beetles which seemed to have adapted to live off of it. It felt and looked like hell.

Rob was in a bad way and considered leaving, but remembered Helen and didn't want to let her down. Like most men in their forties, Rob thought that he still had a chance with Helen, even though he was knee deep in bat poo and his wife was at the top with Helen. The dream never dies, and Rob thought it would be a great story to tell, when he and Helen elope.

Deep down Rob didn't think for a minute that Zak would've made it this far, especially if he was injured in the fall. The quietness was ended with a whiny noise coming from another gap in the cave wall to the right. Rob made his way over and peaked though. Suddenly he could hear the sound of purring, which is a lovely noise with a a vibrant vibration. Rob shone his torch through and could see a group of puma pups. They were beautiful, they were cute and climbing over each other, it was such a beautiful scene. The puma mother must've found a way in so she could use it as shelter for her young. Luckily the mother wasn't around, it was just the perfect pups, they looked inviting, like Rob could jump in and play with them. There was some natural light shining through and the smell was much better, however not perfect.

As Rob clambered closer, he could see Zak's backpack in the corner under some bush. Rob was hoping that Zak had found his way out via the gap the puma's use. That was great news and he couldn't wait to get back and tell his team. Suddenly there was a rustling near the entrance and the adult female puma made her way in, Rob had to duck for cover, his heart was racing and he knew he didn't stand a chance against this huge cat.

The pups were delighted to see their mother and were jumping on her and licking her. It was a natural wonder, which Rob had the opportunity to view for himself. The cats settled down to sleep, so Rob took the opportunity to rest as well. After a few hours the adult cat left the cave, Rob dusted himself off and had a look around with the pups just watching him with curiosity. There were some bones scattered around which Rob thought must've been their lunch, brought to them from their mother. Unfortunately, as he got closer, he noticed they were large bones, and possibly human. Rob then realised that they had eaten Zak, there were signs of ripped clothing in the scrub which looked similar to what Zak was wearing.

Rob gulped and then heard, thud, thud, thud, it was his heart. So many things were running through his mind, firstly, how was he going to get out there alive, secondly, how was he going to tell Helen. It wasn't exactly going to be a hero's welcome that he was expecting. This was seriously going to ruin any chance he had of romance with Helen, but probably just as well as his wife was with her. Rob needed to focus and start thinking with his head, he had to get out of there quickly.

His dilemma was whether he should go back the way he came or try and sneak out of the small cave exit just a few metres ahead. He didn't have long to think about it and didn't want to run into the bats and the guava again, so decided to make a break for it. He dropped anything that would hinder his exit, and with shaking legs and adrenaline running through his body he went for it. After just a minute Rob was free from the cave and could smell the fresh air. The puma was no where to be seen, so he checked his compass and headed for the group.

Rob ran as quickly as he could and saw the group in the distance, there was smoke raising up into the canopy of the forest, he slowed down to a walk and as he got closer, he could hear the group talking. Rob could see Zak, he was sat next to Rob's wife and they were laughing and cuddling. Rob couldn't believe what he was seeing. He entered the camp area and everything went quiet, they stared at Rob in a way that they were really surprised to see him. Rob was confused and asked them what was happening, Zak told a story of him wondering off and getting lost. Eve looked embarrassed, and then Rob saw the tree that had the rope wrapped around it. The rope wasn't there, had they planned on getting rid of Rob with this elaborate story. He couldn't be sure, but the group walked back to the hut.

One by one they entered the hut, Rob heard a rustling noise behind him somewhere in the bush, then he heard a growl. Rob turned towards the hut, but Zak and Eve closed the hut door, locking Rob out. Just as Rob turned back to the jungle the huge puma jumped on him, clamping its teeth around Rob's weak throat, there was no getting out of this and he knew he was done for. With only seconds left to live he could only wonder what had really happened.

The End

Cold Hearted Dennis

He was running for his life, desperately trying to get away from this group of killers. He was fast and athletic but there were many of them. He dived into an alleyway and sprinted, one wrong move, a trip or a slip on the dirty wet concrete and he would've been attacked and killed. The alleyway was narrow and dark, it was the back end of several businesses, so all sorts of items were discarded without a care. He was hopping and sprinting and avoiding every possible life ending obstacle he could.

He got to a 10-foot metal mesh fence and was able to jump up and scramble over. His mortal enemies struggled which gave him time to slip away into the darkness and back to black.
"That was far too close, I need to be more careful", he said to himself.

"He", was Dennis. An unremarkable man to look at, six-foot-tall, boring haircut and plain clothes. The perfect look for a Prince to hide in plain sight. He never did anything remarkable; he didn't want to stand out.

Dennis lived in Brighton and was 230 years old. He didn't look it though. He chose Brighton because he thought his peculiar behaviour wouldn't be seen as too strange there. There was always something happening in the city and Dennis lived in Kemptown, above a historical small theatre.

Life started a long time ago for Dennis, he was born in Copenhagen and was indoctrinated into his family's way of life and culture. Throughout his long life, he had fed on thousands of victims and has made many enemies along the way.

After the death toll was rising in and around Copenhagen, they moved to Stockholm in Sweden. There were many remote communities in Sweden and for years Dennis took what he wanted. Death became a weekly occurrence and covering his tracks was laborious and boring. He was taught by the elders not to be blasé with his actions but blasé is what he became. The secret to a successful family of vampires is to keep together, keep mixing with the mortals to a minimum and not bring any unnecessary and unwanted attention to their community.

Yes, vampires have a community, they don't display a flag but it's there. Much in the same way as the Cosa Nostra, "it's our thing". Their secrets and stories are passed down the generations, along with methods, techniques and escape routes. Relationships were always encouraged through their own community rather than with an outsider. At least that way you're singing off the same song sheet. However, Dennis did fall in love with a non blood sucker in his twenties.

Every decision has a consequence, and having a relationship with a mortal woman can have incredible consequences. The obvious one is that if the female gets pregnant then the child could follow in the mother's or father's footsteps. Either way, it becomes dangerous and difficult.

The woman Dennis fell in love with was ten years older. Her name was Mary and Dennis met her in a morally bankrupt way. Dennis was watching her husband, as he was going to kill him. During the surveillance process to discover the movements of the man, he couldn't stop staring at Mary. She was beautiful with gorgeous long brown hair, she had a very sweet way about her.

Dennis' next move would define him as a person for the rest of his life. A kill is a kill, but he knew that would break Mary's heart. To not kill, he would have to choose another victim, but to kill the man and start a relationship with his wife would be a sinister decision to make. Dennis made the decision that suited him, he chose to kill the king and take the queen in an Oedipus-style situation.

On the day of the kill, he knew the victim's routine, he watched Mary kiss him goodbye as he waited. When the man had started walking through a copse, Dennis took him and once he was fed he buried the body in a shallow grave. A heartless deed, by a cold-blooded killer.

It took some time but Mary eventually gave in to his overwhelming attention and six months after her husband passed, she was now in a relationship with his murderer. Dennis gave everything he could to the relationship and treated her like a princess. Mary eventually fell in love, and they had some amazing times and adventures, but she could not forget her first love. The death of her husband deeply affected her and after ten years with a vampire she eventually made the heart breaking decision to kill herself.

Mary grew suspicious of Dennis' behaviour and eventually confronted him. He was out late and was always cagey with the truth. Dennis denied any wrongdoing, but Mary knew something was wrong. Poor Mary had been battling with depression for years, she didn't trust Dennis. It got to the point that she couldn't take it anymore, so made the tough decision to end it, she hung herself.

Dennis spent the next hundred years travelling through Europe, where he needed time and his own space. His killing spree continued in cities and towns from France to

Russia. He checked in with his family, he even visited his Grandparents in Romania, Jake and Mina in their newly rebuilt castle. Often he would get annoyed when family members tried to get him to settle down with a distant relative, but he wasn't interested. Dennis may not have been Mary's true love, but she was his. Her death crushed him but he only had himself to blame, he was the cause of her suffering.

Love eventually came back into his life. He met Ann through the 'vampire community' and fell in love for a second time. This was when he moved to Brighton. Ann was more subtle in her feeding habits than Dennis, she would pick on the lonely rather than just anyone. They moved to the Kemptown area, it was quirky, fun and most importantly Brighton has a high number of young-blooded homeless people.

For years they enjoyed the south coast; theatre shows, long walks, sharing meals and they even bought a yacht which they kept at the marina. Life was good. Ann was a good influence on Dennis, she made him more thoughtful and respectful of other people's feelings. It took her a long time but little by little she improved him.
Dennis and Ann packed their bags and headed out to sea on their locally moored yacht. This was a new adventure, but also dangerous as opportunities to feed would be limited. They didn't have a set plan, but little did they know that this would be their last adventure.

Favouring the colder weather, they headed towards the North Sea, towards Northern mainland Europe or Scandinavia as options, but they never made it to land again. A lack of experience and preparation made the North Sea a challenging and dangerous place to tackle. It is a shallow rough sea which makes its currents extremely strong and often pulls in different directions.

On their way up North to begin another new life, they were attacked. A sea monster of folklore nightmares had decided that it would take them down to the depths along with thousands of other maritime vessels. The slippery monstrous animal gripped hold of their yacht from every side, Dennis had little in the way of defence. A kitchen knife from the galley was not up to the task. The yacht was being tossed around, left to right, up and down, Ann and Dennis were now experiencing the fear which they usually saved for their innocent victims.

The cold salty water was filling the boat and the monster's tentacles were searching for its dinner. Ann and Dennis were petrified, they clung on to each other, knowing this was their final moments, there was no escape.

The Giant Squid had pulled the yacht down for its final journey. Dennis and Ann had hid in the lower deck knowing that there was no escape. Ann began to cry, Dennis held her tight.
The monster had done its job in the freezing cold water and had destroyed the lives of the two ultimate blood thirsty killers. In Scandinavia, they had hundreds of

frightening stories about this deadly creature. The folklore tales were true, and the two vampires had disappeared forever.

The End

The Beep

Matt just lay there with his eyes tightly closed. "I'm 40, bloody hell!", he contemplated in his head. He thought it sounded old, and his best years were behind him.

"Matt, Matt, come on you're going to be late", said his wife, Abbie.

Where do you go when you peaked as a child?

Matt was a popular kid, great a most sports, especially football, good looking, intelligent, and had a great if not naughty sense of humour. He thought he would never get older; life was a playground. As a kid you get to try new things for the first time, and it feels amazing, new experiences and tackling new challenges.

As he moved on in his teenage years, the pub and nightclubs were the new experience, drinking and smoking was the thing everyone did. Getting drunk was great, but there was a balance, too much and you become ill and the morning hangovers are torturous. He had a large circle of friends from his school in Steyning, but his main group were, Mark, Simon, Dave and Ed. Ed joined their group late as he attended a different school, but Dave knew him as they were in a rock band together.

Eventually everyone has to grow up, and Matt got a job in a marketing. It was never going to stimulate him, but it paid the bills and that's where he met his wife to be, Abbie. They dated for a while and had a few temporary break ups but always got back together. They got married when he was 27, it felt like the right thing to do even though he was young, he was the first out of his friends to tie the knot.

Mark was the only mate that lived nearby, so they met up fairly regularly, there would be the odd football match, family meet up, gigs and even still went to the pub. They had known each other since primary school so they had a lot of history and many funny stories to reflect on. They were incredibly close, but like most men they would never admit it. Mark's relationship got serious, he had his own commitments and after a few years he had children. Everything was ticking along nicely for around five years, until Mark's marriage broke down. He was always a ladies man and couldn't stop himself from flirting. Eventually after he became a father and was not getting what he wanted at home he had an affair. As quite often in these circumstances, it was with a woman he worked with.

Mark was kicked out of the family home and the new woman was married; she didn't want anything more than a bit on the side. Mark had to move back with his parents until he could sort out his own place, but by then he had hit rock bottom. He was drinking hard, and eventually lost his job, he stopped seeing his children and was rude and abusive to people trying to offer any help. Matt was his closest friend and spent more time with him that he could really afford due to his other commitments, but Mark didn't appreciate it. He would ignore his calls, he would refuse to answer the door and when he did, he acting like a victim, and it was everyone else's fault.

This went on for months, and Matt lost patience with him. He hated seeing his oldest friend fall apart but what else could he do. Matt had a loving wife, two beautiful children and a full-time job he had to prioritise, otherwise his life would start crumbling down like an avalanche. He decided to walk away from the friendship. Matt felt like he was the only one putting the effort in and Mark had just given up on life. It was a tough decision, it really upset Matt, but he needed to break free. They had it so good, and Matt felt he had lost a brother, he was in mourning.

Matt deleted Mark's phone number and vowed to his wife that he was moving on and wouldn't put their relationship under any stress like that again. Life continued for him, work progression, husband duties and running around after the children. They had various clubs that they enjoyed so he was often out in the evenings. He missed his youth and the freedom he had, but he wouldn't swap it, or that's at least what he told himself. This carried on for years, and life moves pretty fast when you're busy.

Whilst sat at home one evening after his fortieth birthday, his phone beeped.

He didn't recognise the number, and it said, hi, it's been a long time, can't we meet? Mark.

Matt couldn't believe it; it had been over five years since he last saw Mark. He didn't know what to do. He left it for a few days, then sent a text back.
"Hi Mark, yes it's been five years. How are you?
Mark explained that when it finally dawned on him that he was about to lose everything, he had a decision to make. He contemplated ending it but took the decision to change his ways and push forward. He managed to find work and was back in contact with his children, his wife was willing to give it another go. They decided to meet up in a cafe in Burgess Hill. It was a lovely old-fashioned place with table clothes and oil paintings.

Matt was nervous on the day of the meeting. He was sweating from his brow and wasn't sure what to expect. When he arrived, he could see Mark was already there, he was sat near the window.

He waved as Matt got closer; he looked good. His hair was short and tidy, he had lost the scraggly beard and was wearing a nice shirt. Matt walked up to the table and Mark stood up, they looked at each other whilst time passed in slow motion. Mark smiled his usual cheeky grin that he has been giving Matt since they were five. Mark's eyes swelled with tears of happiness, and he put his hands out to Matt. Matt paused for a second, then smiled and hugged Mark.

People stared at the two grown men, but they didn't care, in that single moment they became best friends again and that was the only thing that mattered.

The End

The Fall and Rise of Love

At the age of 34, everything seemed pretty good for Sebastian Love, he had a decent career, a loving wife and three beautiful children. They lived in a semi-detached four bed house and loved spending time together.

This sounds fairly normal and probably similar for a lot of families. His lovely wife was called Sophie, and their perfect children are called, Benj, Joni and Luna. They were great children and full of fun, they loved football, gymnastics and dancing.

Sebastian rarely saw his friends, not because they had fallen out, more to do with a lack of time and when he did have time, he was exhausted. His work was going well, he wasn't overly ambitious and was happy with a middle management position. He enjoyed parts of his job but found working with some of his colleagues extremely difficult. Some were work shy and very selfish and Sebastian felt like he was carrying the team, but didn't receive the credit he thought he deserved. He felt frustrated and unsatisfied but that was just the way it was.

He thought about leaving and looking for something else, but it would be difficult. His skills were quite specific, and the money was enough for a good standard of living. They all loved a holiday but Sebastian couldn't fully relax because you just can't when you have three children and you're either near a pool or by the sea. One lapsed moment could be disastrous.

When you have these responsibilities, you can't just chop and change, you have to keep going for the greater good. There's a mortgage to pay, household bills and all of the clubs, clothes and toys to pay for. It can get extremely expensive but he loved his family and wanted the best for them. However, he forgot about himself, he neglected his own needs., it's like jumping on a grenade.

Inevitably, Sebastian got into a habit of having a few beers after the children were in bed. Sometimes he would get a bottle of wine or two, this just helped him relax. The only problem was that it was like truth serum to him and when things were on his mind, he let Sophie know. If she'd not done the washing or cooking he would remind her and when she forgot again he would aggressively remind her. Sophie wasn't lazy, she just wasn't as house proud, and the criticism started to get to her, it affected her sleep and her confidence. Click, click, click, poor Sophie felt like she was living with a time bomb.

In Sebastian's mind he was in the right, he worked harder and wasn't appreciated. He felt like he wasn't getting the respect he deserved. Resentment began to creek into their marriage. Discontent can be cruel and stir in the brain and heart like a tornado.

Sebastian had a friend, Mark, who had recently walked out on his family, he just couldn't take it anymore. The pressure got to him, and he needed his own freedom. He was in a low state of mind and if he hadn't left it may have been the end for him. However, everyone including friends, family and colleagues thought he was selfish and just looking out for number one.

 Sebastian didn't want to follow in his friend's footsteps because he had signed a contract with his loyal Sophie. They were married and to him he had to get through this difficult period for the sake of their marriage. He loved his children and the thought of not seeing them every day killed him. He couldn't become a weekend dad. He wanted to hug them at nighttime and see them every day, they meant the world to him. The thought of being that dad who picks them up to go bowling or taking them to Mac Donald's was not for him and the thought of that just crushed him.

Did he still love Sophie?

Sebastian did love and care for Sophie, but he'd fallen out of love with her. He fell in love with a nineteen-year-old girl and now Sophie was in her mid-thirties and a mother of three. She looked different and they had no quality time together. They were a team, raising three children and working hard to afford everything. Sebastian wondered whether the kids would ever realise what they had sacrificed for them. Their happiness was first and foremost, then the wife and at the bottom was Sebastian, he knew it, they all knew it. It's difficult for a man to talk to anyone about their feelings, which is why they sometimes feel they're left with no choice.

The cuddles and hugs began to become less frequent as their relationship became distant. Any conversation was always about the children. Sophie had a part-time job which was fairly demanding as her boss was a tyrant who was ambitious and tried to squeeze every last bit of energy out of her underlings. She was a typical career crazy, single woman without children who lived and breathed her work. Sophie couldn't quit because they needed her income. She had started smoking again, it was the first time since she was twenty-four. It was usually a sign that she was under pressure, but Sebastian would tell her how lucky she was just working three days a week. He failed to empathise.

One day whilst Sebastian was at work he received an alarming phone call from Sophie's aspiring boss. She bluntly said,
"Hi Sebastian, where's Sophie? Her phone is off, and she's not come into work."

This was bizarre, as he didn't have a clue where she was, she'd never missed work. She didn't have many close friends, and her family lived a few hours away. Sebastian made some calls but nobody had seen or heard from her. He left work early to pick the children up from school and was hoping she would also be there, but she wasn't, nor was she at home. Her car had gone and Sebastian didn't know what to do. He couldn't go out looking for her as he had to look after the children. He began to think the worst.

He decided the only option he had was to call the police and report her as a missing person. He felt anxious about it; he'd began to shake. He was still hopeful she would walk through the front door and act as though everything was fine and wondering what all the fuss was about.

He called the police, and they sent over a couple of officers. They were young and treated Sebastian with suspicion. They turned on their body cameras and searched the house and garden. They were thorough, they even checked the loft. Sophie hadn't taken any clothes with her and her toothbrush was still in the bathroom. She would always brush her teeth at least four times a day, it was a little quirk of hers, Sebastian found her little ways cute.

All sorts of things were going through his mind. Had Sophie met someone else? Had she been involved in an accident? Where was she?
His head was in a daze like a fog had descended on it. His chest was pounding, and he began sweating like a criminal with something to hide.

Sebastian then remembered a documentary he had seen on Netflix about a guy in America called Chris Watts. He had been helping the police find his pregnant wife and children. He claimed his wife had left him, but he had already killed them, all because he had met another woman. Sebastian became nervous that the police might think he's murdered Sophie, he was worried they were going to arrest him. His mind was racing, and any sensible thoughts had taken off and headed to Mars.

The police finally left the family home and Sebastian had to answer some difficult questions from his children but eventually got them to bed with some white lies and reassurance.
By the next morning and after a sleepless night there was no news, Sebastian didn't go to work but got the kids ready and took them to school. He didn't know what to do, so he cut the grass and tried to keep himself busy.

In the afternoon he got a call from the police, they'd located Sophie. Apparently, she had slept in her car and a few local residents were concerned for her safety. They had tried to talk to her but she wasn't making any sense. The police told Sebastian that they'd decided to section her as they were worried about her welfare, and they claimed that she'd had a mental breakdown.

Sebastian was so relieved that she was alive but shocked that she had become mentally ill. He went and visited her in the hospital, and she was in complete denial. She wanted to get out but she was in a secure ward and was locked in for at least two weeks.

Sebastian continued to visit her and eventually they let Sophie have an hour or two in the community to see how she coped. This went fine for a few days, but she was missing the children and began talking in riddles again. The doctor said the she wasn't fit to be released for at least another week or two, but she responded badly to the news.

On the next occasion Sophie was allowed out, she was supervised. But time had taken its toll, and she couldn't handle not seeing the children. Social workers didn't want to allow it until the hospital said it was safe.
As Sophie walked to the shops with her nurse, she noticed a taxi dropping someone off at an office. She ran and dived in and then thrust two twenty pound notes in the drivers hand, and told him to drive. He did as he was told and dropped her in her home town, she made her way to her daughter's dance class at the local leisure centre. Sophie stormed in and demanded to see her daughter,

Luna. The instructor had been updated about the situation and refused, Sophie lost it, she saw red and had lost control.

She pushed past the instructor to gain entry, but when she was stopped by another parent she picked up a rock and threw it through the downstairs window. The police were called and Sophie was carted off in the back of a police van in handcuffs. A new low for Sophie and Sebastian. Poor Sophie was back in hospital and Sebastian stopped off at the shop on his way home for a bottle of wine.

This time Sophie was going to be given anti psychotic medication. An injection once a month for the time being. The doctor said they had to monitor to see if the medication would have an effect. Sebastian left it for a few days and then visited her at the hospital. The doctor told him that Sophie could be with them for up to six months, they were really concerned about her.

This news was hard to take, it had a detrimental impact on him. Sebastian was now acting as a single dad, luckily his mother-in-law was able to help out whilst he went to work. The social worker said that Sophie was going to have to show significant improvements in her mental state before they could allow her to move back in.

The six months didn't go smoothly at all, no more breakout attempts but the relationship between husband and wife was suffering. Sophie blamed Sebastian for her breakdown, she told him that his disgruntled behaviour towards her had destroyed her confidence. He defended himself and told her that if she helped out more he wouldn't have lost his temper. He was disappointed with her attitude and actually thought that the household was running much smoother without Sophie.

The arguments went back and forth and ended with Sebastian telling her that she wasn't welcome back. When she was finally released Sophie stayed with her mother, but after a few weeks she realised what a mistake she'd made. She kept calling him to apologise, at first Sebastian didn't want a reconciliation but after a few weeks decided that it would be best for the children to have her back. They needed a mother at home.

Sophie moved back in and at first things were distant as the children were a little weary of her and Sebastian was worried about any flare ups. As time moved on, bad feelings thawed, and things became better. Days out together helped and she began making more of an effort around the house.

They began again and after plenty of talking, they began working things out together, there was a lot of water under the bridge. Sophie had lost her job, which worked out for the best because she was able to find another which was way less stressful. It gave her something to focus on and her boss was older and more relaxed.

Sebastian reflected on the most chaotic year that they had ever had and how quickly relationships and life can hit rock bottom. Their first Christmas back together was extremely special. Sophie had done a wonderful job with the decorations and presents. Sebastian cooked a mountain of food and in the evening with the log fire raging, they cuddled up on the sofa the first. They watched the children playing with their new toys and just looked into each other's eyes and smiled. They knew their life was far from perfect but at that moment, it was.

The End.

The Angry Ghost

James wasn't always a ghost; he was a 34 year old married man with a lovely daughter called

Suzi. James and his family had just moved to Horsham and bought a lovely three-bedroom detached house on the outskirts of the town. It was nice and quiet and had a huge garden. His wife was called Bella, and she was a Primary Schoolteacher. She loved her work, she was put on this earth to look after children, she was so kind and generous with her time.

James was a mortgage advisor, he enjoyed helping people, so did his best to get youngsters on the housing ladder. He was a good husband, a decent provider, and a great cook. He loved taking his time and making interesting exotic dishes and watching guests enjoy and devour them.

Little Suzi was just five years old, a beautiful little brunette, she had long curly hair and was a cheeky confident child. She loved to play and dance; she would try and sing but it was never going to be her million pound ticket. It didn't matter; they loved just watching her little face light up when she was performing was all we needed.

They had everything going for them. There were plenty of jobs to do around the new house, the walls needed a lick of paint, there was a leaky outdoor tap, and the garden was a huge bundle of prickly brambles.

The first job was to tackle the electrics as they were a mess. Certain plug sockets didn't work, and every now and again the power would cut out.

Job number one was a difficult task and needed an expert. Luckily for James, his good friend and best man was a jack of all trades and said he could help out. They had a quote from a few qualified electricians, and they were asking for thousands, but with everything else they wanted they couldn't really afford it and didn't want to get a loan.

Harry came over one weekend with his tool belt which impressed them, especially Suzi, she said he looked like a cowboy, James just called him Woody, from the Toy Story movie. They were joking about buying him a cowboy hat to finish off the look. Harry took the jokes well and after a cup of coffee and a catch up, he went around the house with James to check out the dodgy electrics and made some notes. He wasn't going to charge for his time but there were some materials needed to complete the job. James was really impressed with how much Harry knew and after they'd finished the examination they went off to the DIY shop to pick a few things up. Suzi went with them and loved being swung around on the trolley, she was laughing and screaming, she got on so well with her Uncle Harry.

When they got back, they placed all of the new material in the garage and made a plan for the following weekend to complete the job. Harry guesstimated that it would take around three hours. James didn't have a clue so just agreed and said he'd buy him some beers and a takeaway for afterwards, the deal was done.

Next weekend came around and Harry was at the front door at 10am. Bella was getting Suzi ready for her dance class, Suzi wanted to stay and help but was told that it was too dangerous for her, as electricity can kill if you're not careful. The girls left the boys to it and James was just following Harry about the house trying to be helpful, he was best used for making tea and moving things out of the way. At one stage Harry asked James to drill a small hole, which he managed to muck up. His drill bit was too large, so he had to go and get some filler.

They stopped for lunch and by now the girls had got home. It was sunny so they all sat outside and ate sandwiches and crisps and had a few beers. Around 1pm, Bella took Suzi out to her mothers as they were getting in the way, and the boys just needed some space. Harry had rewired certain rooms and had changed fuses in the fuse box, it was all quite complicated, but he was a fast worker.

Just before he screwed the wall sockets back into place, Harry wanted to make sure everything worked ok, otherwise he'd had to take them all off again. Harry asked James to go into the garage and flip the switch on the fuse box. James was pleased he was being trusted with something so off he went into the garage and walked over to the nice new shiny fuse box. It looked great, Harry had done a terrific job. It was a little high for James, so he pulled over a little stool to get a better reach.

He set up his camera phone to film the big occasion so he could show Suzi and Bella later in the evening. He stood on the stool, opened the see through plastic case and reached in to switch the large red button from down to up. He turned to the camera as he clicked the switch and the electric came on. The garage light automatically turned on for the first time and the excited James went back inside the house to tell his clever friend, Harry.

Harry was busy screwing the plastic wall fixtures back on and they were two extremely proud men. They completed the downstairs fittings and went upstairs to finish the job. They knew that in a few minutes they would be finished and guzzling down some beers in celebration. Everything was working and looking great, other than the main light in the master bedroom. James grabbed a spare bulb and stood on a chair to reach the light fitting. This didn't work either, there was some sort of glitch with it, so James went and made some tea, it helps men think!

Harry took over and pulled out an electric tester pen, it looks similar to a screwdriver, however it lights up if electricity is live. James had finished his cup of tea and wanted to help. Whilst Harry went back over to the light switch, James was trying to be helpful and stood on the chair, he pulled out his screwdriver and shoved it into the light fitting, just as Harry pressed the switch.

BANG

An almighty bang came from the light fitting along with a burst of electrical flames and the whole room was filled with smoke. The incident tripped the power, but not before a huge surge of electricity ran through the metal screwdriver and into James. Harry ran to open the window to clear the smoke, as the room cleared James was lying on the floor shaking. Harry just watched, he didn't want to get too close as he'd heard that electricity can jump a few metres, and he didn't want to be electrocuted. The shock had stopped James' heart, and his blood had stopped circulating around his body. He was unconscious and sadly died on the bedroom floor within a couple of minutes.

James was dead and Harry panicked, he waited for twenty minutes before he called an ambulance. He'd taken his tools and hid them in the boot of his car. Harry wasn't qualified and was worried he could get arrested for manslaughter for the reckless behaviour. Obviously, he didn't want to go to prison, so made the scene look like it was James who was at fault. The truth was, that they were both to blame, one had paid the price with his death and one was still alive.

After death.

Different cultures have various beliefs on what happens after death. Some people believe that a wronged soul can linger on earth to right a wrong.
James died, but didn't go to heaven or hell. His existence continued in a stream of consciousness after the death of his physical body. In short, his soul remained in the place where he died, his house. His soul was invisible and unable to communicate with the living. It took a while for James to get used to his transition, he was now a ghost.

James found himself back in his bedroom, the place where he died. He didn't remember much about that, other than a huge bang and a puff of smoke. However, here he was alone and didn't know what he was supposed to do, he had to come to terms with his new position as a ghost. It was a metamorphosis he didn't see coming.

After his transformation he was alone in the house for a long time. He didn't understand where his wife and daughter were, but they weren't living in the home. James tried to leave but couldn't, he was trapped in the house like a prisoner. The house was pretty much how he left it before his demise.

It was like a bad dream.

A few months later he was surprised when the front door opened. His wife and beautiful daughter Suzi walked in. They had a few bags with them and her father was carrying some boxes of food. Bella looked sad, she looked around the house and sat on a dining room chair. Suzi was running around exploring, she seemed ok, but Bella looked depressed, she'd lost weight and was so pale. Her father was fussing around moving things and unpacking. He said to his daughter, "Just remember Bella, even if a person dies, the relationship between you doesn't die. Nobody will replace James, but only you can save yourself. I love you."

Bella didn't say anything, she just held on to her father like she was a little child again.

James just watched the girls, he loved seeing his little Suzi playing and running around. It was so hard for him; he couldn't hug them or interact, he missed them so much, he just wanted to give them affection. To hold them and tell them he loved them was all he wanted to do, they meant everything to him. Death was cruel and seeing Bella struggling with her new found situation was even harder. She cried all of the time, her mother came and took Suzi out so Bella could grieve in peace. She was popping pills and drinking a lot of wine, she hardly ate.

The following week Bella had a visitor, it was Harry. Bella listened as Harry spoke,
"Bella, I will always be here for you. I will finish the house off, so don't worry about that."
He was consoling her and brought her a gift. It was a huge bunch of flowers, which dominated the dining room, the card read,
"Dear Bella, it's a new start in life and time to move on, I will always be here for you. Love Harry".

Harry's visits became far too regular and as time went by, he was looking more comfortable at the house.
James took great offence to what Harry was doing, and quite rightly. James was gone and Harry wanted to fill the vacant space. After a year of this cuckooing, Harry eventually moved in and they became a couple. James had forgiven

Bella because she had fallen apart and needed support, but Harry was not going to get an easy ride. This behaviour was unacceptable and would not be tolerated.

James was so angry at having to watch what was happening that he wanted revenge, he lashed out and hit a glass and it moved one centimetre. This might sound pathetic, but it was incredibly significant. It drew the attention of Harry, he turned and looked around, but there was no one there.

Not only did Harry play a part in his death, but he had also now taken over his life. He had completely replaced him. Fortunately, he was kind and caring to Suzi and Bella, they were smiling again and Bella was back at work. She looked healthy and was able to function again. Suzi was too young to really understand what had happened and by the age of six she was looking at Harry like a father figure. This destroyed James. It was as though his heart was in a vice and was gradually being squeezed to breaking point.

James was hell-bent on revenge and had convinced himself that he should torment Harry.

James needed to work out a plan to scare Harry off. He was unable to communicate, to touch or to move anything further than a few centimetres, he knew it was going to be difficult.

He started his haunting at a low level, causing disturbances, manipulating objects and appearing in visions. This went on for months and was freaking Harry out. Harry was working hard on the house, decorating, fixing leaks and tidying the garden.

Harry would put something down like a spanner and when he went to pick it back up it had moved. This might sound like a trivial act but when this type of activity was happening twenty times a day, you would start to question your own sanity. He tried to discuss it with Bella, but she didn't believe him.

Over time James was pushing the boundaries and was able to impose a psychological torment, he was able to manipulate the mind of Harry. He was having nightmares, disturbing thoughts and feelings of paranoia from his part in James' death. Even though James had made a stupid error, in the back of Harry's mind he knew he could have prevented it. He also knew that pursuing a relationship with James' vulnerable wife Bella was morally wrong. He had already lost friends over it.

James became obsessed with Harry, his hatred fed his motivation, he became vindictive and dangerous. James moved his revenge up a gear by causing physical harm to Harry. He had attacked Harry's sanity, now he wanted to cause injuries.

James would push glassware off the table when Harry was barefooted. He would fiddle with the settings of his power tools, but most dangerously he would turn the gas hob on, to cause an explosion. He would only do this if the girls were at school and out of the house, his love for them was for eternity.

So many years went by observing his family, seeing them grow, watching them laugh and loving each other, it was a double-edged sword. James loved to see Bella and Suzi happy but couldn't forgive Harry. Watching the man who could have prevented his death weasel his way into his wife's life, watching that bastard live his life, whilst James was trapped in this miserable after death existence.

Eventually, after years of being haunted by the spirit of James, Harry became a shell of his former self. He was paranoid and on medication for his mental health. His guilt played a huge role in his demise and Harry moved out. James just watched the relationship dissipate and continued his aggressive psychological and physical attack, it resulted in Harry giving up after offering everything he had to make Bella and Suzi happy.

After Harry left, James watched Bella sink into depression again, she stopped working and began to blame herself for her own situation. Suzi was a strong child and kept her mother busy at home but deep-down Bella was falling apart.

James had broken her heart for the second time, he had caused this with his terrible besotted jealousy. His persistent pursuit of revenge had backfired, and poor Bella was suffering at the hands of his stubborn stupidity for the last time.

Bella had too many bad memories at the house and decided she couldn't live there any longer. The house was put up for sale and within a few months Bella and Suzi had gone. They had disappeared out of James' death forever and he would no longer be able to watch them grow older. He'd lost everything all over again.

The angry ghost had become bitter with rage. The new residents of his dream house had bought more than they bargained for.
James was set for a long miserable death stuck in the home that was now his eternal prison. It could have been so different, but his ego wouldn't allow it. Hasty emotional decisions led to his downfall. James knew that he should've looked at the bigger picture, but his pride and anger didn't allow it.

Revenge and regretting will never outweigh forgiveness and forgetting.

The End.

The Man Who Fell From Space

As if from nowhere, he awoke on a park bench. He looked around, the sun was just coming up and he felt a little chilly. "Where am I?" he thought. Worse still, "who am I?"

The poor guy did not have a clue. It was as though this was his first day on earth. He didn't even know what he looked like. He could tell from his hands that he was white, he had black jeans on and a large grey coat, but other than that he was none the wiser.

He just sat there and watched as people were rushing through the park to get where they needed to be. A man whizzed by on a bike and a couple of teenagers strolled past. A harassed woman pushing a buggy with a whiny toddler, almost sprinting, went by.

Yet he just sat there. He saw some dogs running around and a squirrel scampering up a tree as though it was being chased. Then the man saw a road and vehicles in the distance. At that point he thought he'd get up and have a look around.

He walked towards the road and the closer he got the louder and busier it became. As he got to the road he stopped and watched as the world was travelling around so quickly. He turned left and walked past a shop window; it showed his reflection. He took a moment to look at himself.

He didn't recognise the person staring back at him, he felt confused and completely lost. He saw an elderly looking man staring back at him, he was average. Average height, average build and had short hair. He couldn't really make out any details.

He felt hungry and could smell food coming from a few shops. He checked his pockets to see if there was any money and he found a small leather wallet. He pulled it out and there was a ten-pound note, nothing else other than a a business card. It read, The Sea Breeze BnB, Chester Road, Brighton. He looked up at the shop signs to see if there was anything that might have a familiar name, but there wasn't. There was a Tattooist a bit further down the road and it said on the window in garish bright green writing, "The Best Tattoos in Brighton".

"Well, that confirms it then, I'm in Brighton", he said to himself. First things first, breakfast. He found a little cafe and ordered a hot sausage roll and a cup of tea. It went down well, and the sound of his stomach rumbling had stopped. He felt better, but then didn't know what to do, he felt like a child that had lost his mother.

He had the address of the Bed and Breakfast but didn't have a map and certainly no phone. He wondered around for a while and saw a few people at the bus stop. He approached a nice-looking lady in her late fifties and asked her if she knew where Chester Road was, she didn't, but a younger man said he knew and pointed him in the right direction.

The problem with Brighton is that it's incredibly hilly, and he was already tired from his morning's efforts. He found another bench and sat down to rest. Within a few minutes a scruffy looking fella sat down next to him. He smelt a bit stale and then clicked open a can of cider. They looked at each other, and the scruffy man said, "Do you want some cider? I saw you looking at the can".

The lost man said, "No thank you, I don't drink, or at least I don't think I drink".

The younger man looked at him for a few moments and said, "what do you mean you don't know if you drink? What's the matter with you?"

The lost man said, "Well, I don't think I've been here before, so I don't know if I drink alcohol or even what my name is".

"What are you talking about? Have you lost your mind? Or did you just drop to earth <u>this morning</u> from space?" Spewed the young man, and he laughed at his own wit.

Looking a bit dazed, the older man said, "I could have, I mean I don't know how I got here. I don't remember anything at all".

The younger man replied with a smile, "In that case, you'll be known as, The Spaceman."

"Oh, very well then, if that's what you think is best", said the older man in a deflated voice. "What should I call you?" The scruffy man replied, "you can call me, Banjo".

That was it, the Spaceman was now his name. After a few more minutes he slowly got up and told Banjo that he was going for a walk up the hill to find Chester Road. Banjo said, "Ok Spaceman, I'll come with you, I have a mate staying up that way".

Off they went very slowly up the hill to find the bed and breakfast. By the time they reached it, both men were out of breath and sat on a garden wall to rest. They looked over at the Sea Breeze BnB and it looked terrible. The paint was peeling off the walls, the curtains were filthy and there was a build up of rubbish in the front yard. However, it wasn't as bad as the neighbours. It had boarded up windows, the front door was broken and hanging off the hinges. It looked like it was ready for a bulldozer.

The Spaceman said, "What a place, this is disgusting, who would live there?"

Banjo smiled and said, "my mate Dave stays in that place", pointing to the run-down derelict house. "It's a squat, people come and go, its chaos, nobody really lives there. My mate Dave has been there for a few weeks, it's a bit of a drug den, but they have some fun parties, last week someone overdosed and died, poor girl".

With that the Spaceman got up and walked over to the BnB, he knocked on the door and a smart woman answered. She looked at him, grabbed his arm, pulled him in and shut the door. Banjo was stunned and knocked at the BnB to see what was happening, but no one answered the door. He waited for a while then shrugged it off and went next door to see Dave. Within a few minutes Banjo and Dave were smoking a joint.

Meanwhile, the Spaceman was dragged into what looked like the lounge. He sat down and two men came in and sat opposite. They stared at him and the taller man said, "Where have you been? You've been gone for weeks." The Spaceman was stunned, he didn't say anything, he couldn't because he didn't have an answer. They repeated the question and just watched him. The

Spaceman, replied, "Do I know you? Is this where I live? Am I in trouble?"
The two men stared at each other, the tall one said, "we'd better take him downstairs".

With that they pulled him up by his arms and guided the old man downstairs. The stairs were dark and smelt of damp, as they got closer to the basement, it stunned the old man. Suddenly it was all bright and shiny, it took his eyes a moment to adjust. It was as though he had entered a new dimension. There were huge touch screen TV's on the walls and people dressed smartly looking busy pushing buttons and speaking into headsets. It was extremely high tech, and the men shuffled him past into a smaller room to the side.

The Spaceman could see the room looked softer and more welcoming, there was a sofa, a small bed and a sink with some cupboards. He felt like he was at the doctor's surgery. He sat on the bed, whilst the other two men perched on the sofa, looking uncomfortable. No body said anything for a few minutes, which was uncomfortable and also surreal. A woman opened the door and was wearing a white three-quarter length coat, she was holding an iPad.

She was in her late thirties, with her hair tied up in a bun, she seemed quite pleasant and asked the old man how he was. He replied in a concerned manner, "I'm fine, but why am I here? Who are you? What's going on?"
She said, "My name is Zara, and I'm here to extract the intelligence you have obtained for us. I know you have a lot of questions, but your memory should be back soon. First of all I need you to take some tablets, they will help you."
With that, Zara, pulled the tablets out of her top pocket and went over to the sink to pour a glass of water.

The Spaceman was in a difficult position, firstly, he didn't know who he was, where he was or what he was doing, and secondly, he didn't know if he could trust these people that he'd just met. After plenty of reassurance and encouragement from Zara, he took the tablets and lay down on the bed. The two men left the room and Zara sat down and was tapping away on her iPad. Within a few minutes, the Spaceman began to hallucinate, he was seeing all sorts of colours flying from the walls and around the room, an owl appeared in the corner and just stared at him, it then flew towards him with its talons out and just before contact was made he was out, completely unconscious.

When he awoke from his drug induced sleep, he was alone. The lights were dulled, and it was dead silent. The Spaceman got off the bed and walked over to the sink, he poured himself a drink and sat on the sofa. He still felt a little dazed, so took a few minutes to hydrate and wake up. Once he felt more stable he stood up and walked over to the door, it was locked. He tried to force it, but there was no chance of opening it. He knocked and said, "hello", nothing, so he tried again, nothing, so he went and sat back down on his sofa.

Around an hour later, the door opened, Zara walked in.

"Well, Mr Smith, you're back with us. Now we need to debrief you. Let's take you into Interview Room 3, come on."

The Spaceman followed Zara into the bare room, it just had a desk and three chairs, no pictures, no signs, nothing. They sat down opposite each other and Zara looked at him for around thirty seconds before she said, "Mr Smith, tell me about the Wrecking Crew? What did you find out?"

The Spaceman replied, "I didn't find anything out, I have no idea what you are talking about, what's going on?"

"This is most odd Mr Smith; you should have your full memory back by now. You're not holding anything back from us, are you? These people are incredibly dangerous and we're expecting an attack ASAP. If we don't stop this group, they will kill somebody, they're reckless."

Zara said in a slightly concerned manner.

"Can I go please? I have a friend waiting for me," asked the old man.

"No, you can't, you will wait here until you tell me everything you know about the Wrecking Crew. Just tell me". Zara was clearly getting annoyed and impatient, her voice was becoming higher pitched and louder, she was on the verge of screaming.

Zara made a quick call, the two men walked in and grabbed the Spaceman, both were either side of him and they took him into another small room, it looked like a laboratory. It had a CT scanner, which dominated the room, he was motioned to lay down on it and not move. They started the scan which was making all sorts of noises and moved around his head, it was loud and scary. Once it had finished, they told him to wait. They took blood and hair samples and even took his fingerprints.

Zara came back in after a few hours, she said, "Unfortunately, the results have been analysed and the damage to your memory could be irreversible. We haven't got time to waste waiting to see, so we're going to send you on your way. Whatever you do, do not speak of this place, otherwise we will come for you."

"Ok, but who are you, who's Mr Smith", said the Spaceman.

Zara, snapped back, "We're from a government agency, we keep people safe, that's all you need to know".

The Spaceman was unceremoniously kicked out of the BnB or safe house, or whatever it was, it certainly wasn't his home. As he left, Zara said, "get yourself to the council, it's about fifteen minutes away, head down the hill, it's a huge building, they might be able to help you". There was a sound of a banjo coming from the squat as he walked off, he thought about knocking for his new friend but decided to leave it, it looked intimidating.

The Spaceman followed her directions and found the grand council building, he told them that he didn't know who he was, and he was recently kidnapped by secret agents. The kindhearted housing officer, who had intended on helping the Spaceman with temporary accommodation, realised that he wasn't safe to be left alone, he wasn't making any sense, so called the police who eventually arrived and sectioned him, for his own safety.

They took him to the local mental hospital where he was assessed by a nurse. They gave him his own small room and reassured him that the doctor will come and examine him the following day. He was fed, given clean clothes and slept.

At first Dr Brown thought the Spaceman had a simple case of amnesia. Maybe due to a bang on his head or possibly a seizure due to a tragic event which his brain was trying to delete. However, the more he spoke with the Spaceman the more he was intrigued and fascinated by what he had to say.

After a few sessions the Spaceman began to talk about the planets and the solar system. He had a deep knowledge of the 8 planets,

290 moons, 1.3 million asteroids and about 3900 comets. He knew their names, their routes, he even knew locations of some black holes. It was extraordinary.

Doctor Brown was convinced his new patient was a lecturer at a university or worked at the UK Space Agency. He made the relevant calls but nothing, he wasn't even listed as a missing person with the police.

The Spaceman was his usual self, mostly just spent his days watching TV or reading. He spoke to other patients but on the whole, he kept himself to himself in between treatments. He still didn't know who he was, and couldn't explain his incredible knowledge, he was turning into the scientist Dr Brian Cox.

Then one day, the Spaceman spoke about leaving and told the Doctor that his friends were picking him up. The Doctor questioned this and told him that he wasn't ready to be discharged. Then the Spaceman said something that shocked the Doctor, he said,

"My friends don't need your permission; they will take me <u>this Friday</u>. No one will be able to stop them".

The Doctor had so many questions, but the Spaceman casually walked back to his room without saying another word. In fact, the Spaceman didn't say another word for the rest of his stay.

<u>On Friday morning</u> the Doctor got into work early and rushed to the Spaceman's room.

It was empty. The bed was made and there was no sign he had ever been there. The doctor ran to the dining hall, he also spoke to staff. No one had seen him since <u>Thursday night</u>. He checked CCTV, nothing. The Spaceman had disappeared, like the invisible man.

He didn't leave a trace, other than a small business card for The Sea Breeze BnB, Chester Road, Brighton.

Six months later, there was an explosion at a university building, the Wrecking Crew had targeted it due to the experiments on animals. They'd targeted the logistical aspects of the university; they wanted to destroy the IT systems.

The Wrecking Crew used far too many explosives and took out the whole building, killing one person and maiming another. Zara and her team were working day and night trying to find out who and where these guys were. The injured man was in a serious way and the doctors wouldn't let anyone near him for fear of contamination, he had 40% burns and internal bleeding. He was going to need constructive surgery to repair his injuries.

The dead man was taken to the coroner, he had no identification on his person, his DNA had not been traced, but he had a few tattoos. The police released pictures of these in the media, trying to get a family member or a friend to come forward to identify him. The tattoos were of a Celtic cross on his arm and a banjo on his chest.

The injured man was in intensive care for two weeks, the police were eventually able to test his DNA and fingerprints in order to identify him.

It was Mr Smith, the **Spaceman**.

Months later, when the Spaceman was well enough to talk, he had a visit from Zara. Amazingly he had regained his memory, he wished he hadn't. He had a tragic tale to tell.

At 17, he moved to the US, after his father got a job with NASA. He had a great life, he became a Biochemist, he married a beautiful woman called Sara and they had a wonderful son called Zak. Last year, Sara and Zak went out for dinner, they were caught up in a robbery and both were shot and killed. Mr Smith had a breakdown and couldn't live with the pain he was suffering; it was too much to bear for him. He decided to return to England and get away from the memories.

He realised when he got back to England that he didn't have a lot to come back for. His parents had died, he was an only child, and his friends had long disappeared from the area. He stayed in a small hotel in the Kemptown part of the city, he had some money so didn't really need to work, he didn't know what to do with his days.
 He began to find a routine of going for a walk after breakfast, he was into photography so loved taking pictures of the beautiful historical buildings as well as the run down graffiti covered slums. It was all fascinating to him, taking pictures during different times of the day would give him a completely different image, the colours would change, the people rushing around was always so different.

On one of his walks, he was approached by a woman, Abbie, she was pretty and dressed in hippie attire. She was nice and they made small talk about the weather and where it was good to eat out. A few days later they met again, and it became more regular, it got to the point she accompanied him for his photographic tours, they became friends.

After a while, Abbie began to ask more personal questions and spoke about her hatred of animal cruelty. She mentioned PETA and said that there was a movement in Brighton. She discovered that he was a Biochemist, this fascinated her as it gave her an insight into the scientific world. Their friendship became stronger, and he opened up about his wife and his son. He wanted to hold on to this information as it was so personal but once he started talking about his love for them and how they still impacted his thoughts almost every second of the day, he couldn't stop, it flowed like his tears. It was amazing, Abbie proved to be a great listener, she paid attention and let him remember. She was a humanist as well as an animal rights activist.

After what seemed like hours, Mr Smith thanked Abbie and they hugged. She held him tightly, he cried, for a moment he completely lost control of himself and just wept like a child. He felt absolutely exhausted and went back to his room and lay down. He noticed a small envelope that was slide under his door. He opened it and it was a business card, which read, The Sea Breeze BnB, Chester Road, Brighton, he couldn't understand why he had been sent it, so just placed it in his wallet, lay down and fell asleep.

During the night, he tossed and turned and wept some more, he was heartbroken. His heart actually broke, and he had a terrible seizure, nature has a funny way of hitting the reset button. He fell out of bed and banged his head on the bedside table. Luckily he was still dressed, he had lost all sense and hobbled out of the hotel, walked to the park and lay down on a bench.

Abbie had been feeding her informative chats with Mr Smith back to her friends, her friends just so happened to be activists in an exclusive group called the Wrecking Crew.

At this point they were just out to cause annoyance, leaflet drop, display posters and to cause disruption. All low level ways of spreading the message to the people about animal cruelty. Mr Smith was seen as someone who could be useful and advise them further into how the scientists work with the animals and how they could stop the process. After Mr Smith opened up to Abbie, she realised how damaged he was. She was dead against the group using him, but it was too late.

The next thing he knew, Mr Smith had woken up on a bench in a park in Brighton. He had forgotten everything, his mind had shut down. This is when Banjo got involved, he was the next step in the recruiting process. Banjo wasn't aware of the Intelligence Department at The Sea Breeze BnB, but he waited and watched. When Mr Smith was sectioned, Banjo had an associate working security at the hospital, the planned breakout was easy. The CCTV was deliberately switched off, and Mr Smith was led out of the front door <u>at 3am</u> in the morning, without any resistance at all. Banjo was there to pick him up and took him to a friend's house, where he was groomed and indoctrinated into the Wrecking Crew.

After years of low level disruption, the Wrecking Crew had plans to make a headline attack on the use of defenceless animals for science at the university. The plan was to blow up the IT server which would set the university back years. A group of four were tasked with the operation, including Mr Smith and Banjo who was leading the team. Due to their lack of knowledge of explosives, Mr Smith put together a chemical reaction which would be enough to cause the damage they'd required.

Unfortunately, Mr Smith had misjudged the amount needed and had a "you're only supposed to blow the bloody doors off" moment. The chemical reaction took out the IT server but had a domino effect on the building and the whole place came down. Banjo and Mr Smith were caught in the explosion, Banjo died and Mr Smith lived to tell the tale.

Due to Mr Smith's mental health issues, he wasn't prosecuted due to his age and diminished responsibilities, he was put on a care order to see out his days in a controlled care home. He only lived another two years. Abbey continued to visit him, and on occasions brought her son along to visit, he looked just like Banjo, but Mr Smith never asked and Abbey never confirmed it.
The Spaceman suffered with his long-term injuries, his depression and his old age. He was looking forward to death and had stopped taking his medication. On his final day on earth, he wrote a quote in his diary,

"The only real battle in life is between hanging on and letting go" (Shannon L Alder).

The End.

Printed in Great Britain
by Amazon

62896411R00082